A Temptress in Tartan

A TEMPTRESS IN TARTAN

All the King's Men

Gerri Russell

Diana,
It is a great pleasure to
know you and work with you!
Best,
Gerri
Russell

TULE
PUBLISHING

Dedication

To my Lady Lairds. I appreciate each of you so very much.

PROLOGUE

Falkland Palace, Scotland
August 1st, 1592

E LIZABETH RUTHVEN STOOD at the edge of a cliff that fell several hundred feet straight down. A short distance from her booted toes was a thin, whisper-sheer cascade of water that tumbled over the broken lip of the precipice, spraying transparent, rainbow-hued mist onto the rocks below. An updraft of wind swooped over her from the moorland. In the distance, like an amber jewel set in a sea of green, was Falkland Palace.

Tears flooded Elizabeth's eyes, falling to her cheeks momentarily before they were dried in the wind. King James VI and Queen Anne had brokered a truce between the Ruthven and the Douglas clans by forcing her to marry Lachlan Douglas on the morrow—a man she had never met, but whom she was born to detest.

A sad smile came to Elizabeth's lips. It wasn't every day a girl turned nineteen. Yet on her birthday, tomorrow, she would be forced to marry a man she did not love and did not even know. A man her father had talked about her whole life as evil incarnate. And now she was supposed to marry this . . . demon . . . when her heart belonged to another?

How did the king and queen imagine this arrangement would succeed? Two sworn enemies with no common ground? The queen had tried to assure Elizabeth that her bridegroom was not evil, and that he was indeed educated, civilized, a gentleman, and a warrior. The king had simply scowled at her and demanded she do as she'd been bid.

Had she been born male, she would not be in this position, she reflected bitterly as she took a look at the empty void below her feet. She wanted Roland Carswell in spite of his faults. She'd been in love with him for the past five years. Elizabeth released a ragged sigh. But she was not male, no one cared that it was Roland she loved, and it did no good to wish for what could not be.

Instead, she would be terrified to be alone every single day with the man she would be forced to marry, waiting for the moment when the bloodshed between their two families erupted anew. And it would continue no matter what the king or queen did to stop it. The hatred between their two families ran too deep for the fighting to end. Which was why she had come to this ledge. Her death would at least prevent her from sacrificing herself on the altar of supposed peace. Elizabeth shifted up on the balls of her feet, ready to jump.

"Is it really as terrible as all that?"

Elizabeth startled at the unexpected sight of a man not ten paces from her on the cliff's ledge. How had he managed to get so close without her noticing? Then another thought struck her. Was he here to harm her before she could harm herself?

He did not have the ragged look of a thief or a vagrant about him; his white muslin shirt was clean and well fitted to his muscular chest and his breeches were well tailored. His boots were of the finest leather and polished to a high shine. The fading sunlight caught and caressed the man's features, limning his cheeks and throat with light and tipping his eyelashes with gold. His blue eyes were filled with concern as he inched closer to her.

Blue eyes that seemed ever so familiar. "Stay where you are," she warned.

He paused and looked over the edge of the cliff before returning his gaze to hers. "It's a long way down. Before you plunge over the side and to your doom, would you care to talk about what's bothering you?"

"What's there to talk about?" Elizabeth said with her fists clenched as tightly as her jaw. "Besides, why do you care?"

They stared at each other for a heartbeat before he replied, "It would be a shame to spoil something so perfect as you."

Heat came to her cheeks as she looked away, needing a reprieve from his calm, unnerving stare.

The young laird took three steps toward her until her gaze shifted back to him. He was beside her, an arm's length away. Elizabeth frowned down at the emptiness below her.

She wobbled slightly before she sucked in a startled breath and stiffened, stopping her forward momentum.

The blond-haired man met her frown with one of his own. "At least you have the sense to be frightened."

Elizabeth opened her mouth to argue, but realized he was right. She was frightened, not only of leaping to her death, but also of marrying a stranger. In order to avoid acknowledging the truth, she changed the subject. "May I ask what you are doing out here in the middle of nowhere?"

He studied her for a long moment before he said, "The Lomond Hills are not 'nowhere' and nay, you may not."

Despite her precarious situation, her temper flared and her skin warmed beneath the boldness of his gaze. "If you are going to be rude, then please leave. I would rather not die feeling flummoxed and flighty."

"You are lucky I am here and not someone who will take advantage of this situation—someone with more time and fewer scruples."

"You flatter yourself, sir, if you think you could so easily steal my virtue from me."

"I made no claim to your virtue or anything else." That calm, unnerving gaze of his held her in its grasp long enough for a flush to spread down her throat. His gaze followed to where the damask of her gown molded over her breasts. His eyes were the same brilliant blue as the sky. They held her in check and she had nowhere to look but into their depths.

It wasn't until she felt his arm brush against her back and

pull her toward him that she realized just how deeply entranced she had allowed herself to become. She drew a startled breath. "Let me go."

He held her captive in his arms, facing him. "Only if you promise to remove yourself from this ledge and allow me to return you home with your virtue intact."

He was so close—close enough that she could smell both sunshine and a slight hint of cloves on his skin. She watched as the wind pressed his crisp muslin shirt against his chest and broad shoulders, hinting at a muscled physique beneath. "How dare you," she stammered, shocked by how affected she was by his nearness. Never had she had such a response to any man before, not even Roland.

"You have a lot of fight left in you for one who was willing to leap from that ledge a few moments ago."

"I will fight you with my last breath if you do not let me go," she said tartly. He edged closer, and Elizabeth felt the heat of his eyes rake her again.

"I need your promise you will not leap."

"I do not make promises to strangers."

"Then I shall hold you until you do." His roguish smile brought out a dimple in his right cheek. "Although the longer we remain like this, the more my thoughts drift to other things that could happen between a man and a woman alone in the wilds of Scotland."

"You wouldn't . . ." But even as she returned a defiant stare, she knew she was entirely at his mercy. This man was not like her clansmen who blindly followed her father's lead. This man thought for himself and didn't appear to be one to play by any rules but those of his own making. He was far stronger than she, and it appeared just as stubborn.

Elizabeth frowned. Whether she wanted to admit it or not, she found him intriguing. There was something reckless about him that made her heart pound within her chest and sent her blood singing through her veins. She tried to pull away, but he held tight. "Why are you doing this? It does not concern you."

"Today's anxiety will only be a memory of a bad day tomorrow. Nothing in your life could be so bad that you would have to take your own life to avoid it."

Her frown deepened. Was the stranger right? If she died, then Lachlan Douglas wouldn't have to marry her either. And her father would no doubt blame her—but the feud would continue.

Elizabeth drew a thoughtful breath. Would it be better for her to live and force Lachlan to want to find a way out of their marriage instead? Could she stir up enough trouble until *he* would do anything to be rid of her? Or, she could always kill him instead. Her father would approve of that tactic. Elizabeth brought her gaze back to the man who held her and said the words he wanted her to say, "I promise not to harm myself."

"That is a relief," he breathed, then brought his hand up, winding an errant tendril of her brown hair around his finger.

Her pulse raced. "What are you doing?"

"Remembering you and this moment. Is that all right?"

"Nay." She felt breathless, shaky, confused. She did not know this man, and yet something deep inside her felt as if she did.

He didn't stop stroking her hair. In the silence, she heard their breathing as it mingled with the wind that ebbed and flowed around them. She heard the pounding of his heart, though it was probably only her own. He held her so close she could feel the heat of his body, and smell the musk of his skin.

Something dark and unreadable crossed his gaze as he released her hair and brought that same finger to stroke the skin of her cheek. "You are so beautiful. Whoever he was who sent you up here on the ledge should be strung up by his thumbs for making you feel so hopeless."

His words ran over her like honey. She swallowed, suddenly hot and flushed and a little faint. "What makes you think a man is the cause of my troubles?"

"Isn't it always a man behind a woman's sadness?" His startling blue eyes connected with hers. There was some emotion in them, something uncertain and yearning. That emotion pulled at her, filling her with an overwhelming urge to move closer, to lift her face to his.

His eyes held her in watchful suspension as his head drifted lower, his lips nearing her own.

She held her breath. His hands drifted to the narrow indent of her waist and against her better judgment, she closed her eyes, waiting for his kiss.

Instead, a sharp whistle vibrated in the air. She felt herself being lifted. Her eyes flew open as a white horse came to an immediate halt beside the man. The pressure of his hands increased as he lifted her higher, then unceremoniously settled her atop the horse. He took a half-step back. "This is for the best."

A stab of regret pierced her chest. Before she could object, he slapped his hand across the horse's flank. She jerked back in the saddle as the horse spirited her down the path at the edge of the cliff to safety below.

Once on the moorland, the horse did not stop. The beast continued racing toward Falkland Palace and her bridegroom awaiting her there. Why had she not met the stranger on the cliff before today? Perhaps then the two of them could have explored the palpable attraction between them without regret. Perhaps they still might if she could turn the horse around and go back to him and convince him otherwise.

Elizabeth leaned forward, trying to gather the loose reins in her hands, but failed as she was forced to hold on to the saddle itself to stay upright. Her skirts whipped around her legs and her cheeks were on fire at the memory of the stranger's arms locked around her, his fingers in her hair. At least she would have the memory of her brief encounter with a stranger to hold in her heart as she married a man who could only ever be her enemy.

The sun was setting as the horse entered the palace gates as if knowing exactly where to return her. At the sight of her, a tall and lanky stable boy she recognized as one of her father's own ran up to greet her. "Milady, 'tis good ye are returned," Richie said, his brows drawn together with concern. "Yer father is in the palace, and he's displeased that ye weren't here tae greet him." The lad caught the reins of her horse and brought her to a stop. "Ye best go inside now afore he works himself into one of his rages." He offered her a hand down.

"My thanks, Richie," Elizabeth said with a nod of appreciation before heading to the doorway that would take her to the great hall where her father no doubt waited to berate her for inconveniencing him. She hadn't taken two steps before that feeling of fear she'd tried to escape returned. She drew a breath, forcing it back, as she had for the last three weeks since she'd learned about her betrothal to her enemy. Instead, she concentrated on the sound of her footfalls on the gravel in the drive as she made her way inside.

She looked about the chamber hoping and praying to see a familiar dark-haired man who had been gone from her life for months now, but her beloved Roland was nowhere in sight. Instead, as soon as she entered the great hall, her father turned toward her.

Donald Ruthven's features hardened as he strode to her side. Anger sparked in his eyes. The man was not the clan leader, but he had been playing the role for many years. His brother left a son behind who would take control of the clan in the future, but at fifteen he was too young for such responsibility. Her father had only been too happy to lead the Ruthvens in the young laird's stead. "Where have you been? Do you not know how dangerous it is for you to go outside this palace alone?"

At her hesitation, he stepped a hairsbreadth from her face, trying to intimidate her. "Answer me, foolish girl. Where have you been? They say you have been gone for hours."

Elizabeth tensed, but held her ground. "I needed to clear my head, so I took a walk," she answered a little more defiantly than she would have three weeks ago. He did not need to know how far she had walked or what her true purpose had been. Such knowledge would only make him angrier.

"A walk?" he sneered. "The Douglas bastards could've found you and killed you. Then where would we be? If you don't get married, then we do not receive the money that's been promised us."

"Three weeks ago, you didn't want me to marry the Douglas at all," Elizabeth stated boldly. Something about her meeting with the stranger in the Lomond Hills suddenly gave her a strength she hadn't possessed when she left the castle this morning.

Her father's face darkened. "That was before the king

and queen withheld our funds until you are wed." His lips curled in a satirical smile. "'Tis after the wedding when we'll work to free you from that bond. For then the king and queen cannot punish us for not holding up our end of this vile bargain."

Unable to maintain her bravado, Elizabeth took several steps back, putting some space between herself and her father. "I shall play my part. Have no fear of that, but until the wedding, please leave me in peace." With that, she turned and fled from the room. They would see her tomorrow morning when she could no longer avoid her duty. Until then, she had no desire to be near her kinsmen who put her in this awkward position in the first place, or to see her bridegroom when he arrived at the palace. Let her father fret a little until he received his bribe from the king and queen, and let her bridegroom wonder about who he would be marrying until the appointed time.

CHAPTER ONE

THE WEDDING WAS over before it even began. Or at least that's what it felt like to Elizabeth. She paid no attention to the king and queen sitting near the altar, but only as if they were dolls in a set piece, nor did she quite note any of the other guests gathered in the chapel. From the moment she entered the chapel and saw the man waiting there for her near the minister, her brain shut down, her knees went weak, and nothing around her seemed real as she got her first glimpse of her bridegroom's startling blue eyes.

There was no mistaking those eyes, no misreading the slight curl on his lips that inched higher when he saw the shock register on her face. Though he was dressed more formally now in a fine linen shirt and kilt in the Douglas colors, it was the same rogue who had stopped her from leaping off the ledge in the Lomond Hills yesterday.

Sweet Mary! For a brief moment yesterday, she'd actually considered turning herself around and willingly going back to indulge in a momentary liaison with his man.

Her enemy.

A man to whom she was now married! The vows were

said, the blessing given, all while she continued to stare, transfixed, at him. When he bent to kiss her, whatever spell she had been under shattered and she took a step back. "Why didn't you tell me you were Lachlan Douglas?" she asked, fighting hard to control not only the shock, but the indignation that coursed through her in equal measure.

Lachlan's gaze narrowed on her face. "I was not trying to be deceptive," he whispered for her ears alone. "Until a few moments ago, I did not know you were Elizabeth Ruthven."

"I am. And we are enemies." Elizabeth was only dimly aware of the wedding guests in the chamber as all her attention remained focused on the man before her.

"Are we?" Drawing her closer, Lachlan embraced her as he had yesterday—molding her to the hard contours of his body. "Honestly, I am not displeased it is you."

A mindless drumming flowed through her as she lowered her gaze a fraction and it was no longer his eyes that held her transfixed, but the sensual curve of his mouth—a mouth that was descending toward hers even as his hand slid up from her waist to cradle the nape of her neck.

His lips touched hers, and the shock trembled through her body. A protest lived and died in an instant as she could not summon the strength or the wit to pull away. All her senses became centered around the featherlight pressure of his mouth. She clenched her fists at her sides, prepared to endure what she must when he suddenly pulled back. He stepped away, as though he were suddenly done with her.

"'Tis done. A Douglas and a Ruthven are married." Lachlan's voice was hard as he turned to the king and queen. "Just as you demanded."

"You have our gratitude," the king replied. "Since your families are now joined, I trust this will put an end to the feud that has plagued all of us for years."

Elizabeth's lips twisted in a mirthless smile. *Trust?* How would she ever be able to trust the man who was now her husband?

As though sensing the direction of her thoughts, he turned back to her and said, "I promise to keep my vows to you, Elizabeth."

"The promise of a Douglas."

"I keep my word."

"A vile warrior, but not a liar," she taunted.

He frowned. "I was forced into this marriage just as you were, but I shall never lie to you. You can trust me on that."

She hugged her arms around herself, trying to stop the shivering that attacked every limb. "I trust very few people in this world and I doubt you will ever be one of them."

He said nothing, yet he continued to gaze at her with a strange, searching appraisal—as though he were looking into her soul. Then he abruptly turned away, addressing the king once more. She leaned forward in order to hear better what he said when she suddenly startled to see her father beside her. His bloodshot eyes narrowed. "Perhaps this won't be such an ordeal for you after all," he said, his voice cracking with anger. "You seemed to enjoy that bastard's kiss."

Elizabeth stepped back from her father as both Lachlan and the king turned toward her. "I was doing my duty. Isn't that what you asked of me?"

"You have fulfilled your duty. The vows are said and the marriage complete." His angry gaze connected with King James's, then shifted back to Lachlan's. "My daughter now falls under *your* protection. If anything happens to her—"

"Nothing will happen to her," Lachlan interrupted, causing the tension in the room to increase even more as he stepped closer to her father, towering over him by a full foot in height. "I will see Elizabeth is safe and that she prospers from this arrangement thrust upon us both."

"You so swear?" her father asked, his voice hard. His eyes harder.

"I swear," Lachlan replied with an edge to his voice.

Her father's frosty gaze narrowed with contempt and disgust a heartbeat before he stepped back, and with the other Ruthvens in attendance at the wedding, turned and left the room.

Elizabeth's heart thundered in her chest. She bit down on her lower lip, needing the pain to help stop the flow of tears forming in her eyes as a feeling of abandonment suddenly came over her. Feeling alone was not a new sensation for her. She'd never really had a place where she'd belonged, even in her own clan. And still, the sensation cut deep. This was her new life now—a captive surrounded by her enemies. Trying to regain her equilibrium, she allowed herself to be escorted to the wedding breakfast that had been set up in the great hall. When Lachlan pulled out a chair for her to sit at the head table, she slid into it and folded her trembling hands on her lap as he took the seat beside her. She would not allow her new husband or any of his kin to see the anxiety that rocked her every nerve and muscle.

Instead of trying to engage her in conversation while the palace's servants regaled them with a repast of bread, fruit, oats, fish, boar, and wine, Lachlan simply watched her with an occasional tug of his lips.

When she could stand it no longer, she faced him fully and asked, "Have you nothing to say?"

"What would you have me say? Should I ask after your comfort? Do you require refreshment other than what is before you?" he asked in an accommodating tone that only fired her ire.

She drew a tight breath. "I require nothing other than to be released from what has been forced on me."

"Nothing was forced on either of us. We both willingly agreed to this arrangement." He frowned. "Unless you consider my persuading you to change your mind yesterday coercion."

Heat came to her cheeks at the memory of her momentary weakness. "Nay," she replied, feeling some of her anxiety drain away. "I am glad you stopped me from making a mistake. While I am not pleased to be your wife, I am better off alive as you so righteously pointed out in the midst of yesterday's drama."

Lachlan leaned back in his chair. "Is that a thank you I heard jumbled up in all of those words?"

Elizabeth's cheeks flamed. Why did he have to be so annoying? "Aye."

"Aye, what?" He frowned. "I might believe you were sincere if you actually said the words."

The heat in her cheeks reached a searing level as she brought her gaze to his. "Thank you for interfering in my life yesterday."

His lips pulled up in a half smile that brought out the dimple in his right cheek. "Since that is all I am likely to get from you, I will take it." He paused. "You are welcome."

That dimple did strange things to her insides. With an effort, Elizabeth pulled her gaze away and added, "Do not interfere in my life again. I will not thank you next time."

He laughed. "My dearest wife, I intend to interfere in your life every single day until death do we part. And as I promised your father, that death will be of natural causes many years from now."

The great hall hummed with conversation and laughter from those gathered to celebrate their joining. The joviality of the guests was a sharp contrast to the bleakness in Elizabeth's heart. "You intend to put up with me for that long?"

Lachlan's eyes were intent on hers, his face solemn. "I will consider it a challenge and an honor."

Elizabeth's mouth went dry. "How can you say such? I am your enemy."

"You are my wife."

Elizabeth set her fork down after a few bites. "You think after decades of fighting it will all simply vanish because we are now wed?"

Lachlan's gaze connected with hers. A flash of memory sparked. There was something so familiar about those eyes. She remembered those eyes from a time in her past—long before those moments on the cliff.

His gaze narrowed on her and the memory slipped away. "This feud between the Ruthvens and the Douglases started before either of us were born," Lachlan said. "I was caught up in the bloodshed fourteen years ago with my parents' deaths. I've already lost everything, Elizabeth. What more can the Ruthvens take from me . . . unless we have a child?"

A slow flush crept up her neck as her thoughts suddenly turned toward other things. Until that moment she had forgotten all about what came next. The marriage bed. She eyed him uncertainly now, rubbing her suddenly damp palms on the fabric of her gown, her heart thudding. "My laird, you cannot, we cannot . . ." Her stomach tightened at the thought of bedding her husband.

"What is it, Elizabeth? Are you afraid of what happens between a husband and wife?"

She sucked in a breath, afraid now to say what she must. She looked away, and gathering her courage, blurted out,

"They might have forced me to marry you, but I will not rut with you. I will not give you bairns."

All around them the room suddenly silenced and all eyes turned their way. The king stood abruptly; his features suddenly dark. "What is this?" His voice was fierce. "You will bear a child with this man. I command it."

Elizabeth stood and squared her shoulders. "I mean you no disrespect, Your Grace, but this is not something you can command. If it were, there would be a babe in your own arms by now."

A collective gasp sounded all around her.

The queen's cheeks turned scarlet. The king's eyes blazed as he came toward her. He raised his hand to strike. "How dare you. You'll pay for that—"

Lachlan shot to his feet. "Stop, Your Grace." His voice held steely menace. "It does not serve you to lose your temper."

The king stopped and drew a sharp breath as his furious gaze moved from Lachlan to Elizabeth. He dropped his hand and took a step back as his anger ebbed. Finally, once more in control, he raised his chin and said, "The queen and I thought perhaps we were doing something great for Scotland by joining your two families. But now I wonder if we were foolish, or even a little mad to think such an act might solve this problem."

"Only time will tell," Lachlan replied in a flat tone.

"Aye," the king agreed. "That it will."

"With your permission, Your Grace," Lachlan said. "I believe it is best if Elizabeth and I depart for Whittingehame Castle with all due haste. We have much to discuss and many issues to settle between us that would be better handled in private."

"Agreed. I do not envy you that task," the king replied as his gaze narrowed on Elizabeth. "You have our blessing to depart, but before you do, I have something for the two of you. Perhaps it might help to guide your lives together." The king moved back to the queen's side then returned with a thick book, the pages gilded and bound between a hard leather cover. He held the gift out to Lachlan.

"A Bible?" Elizabeth asked.

Lachlan's eyes widened. "You can read?"

Elizabeth stiffened. "Of course. My mother taught me when I was young."

"Good," the king said. "Then you will both be able to use this. It is a wedding gift from the queen and myself. 'Tis a prototype of a new Bible I am having translated to try and make the word of God more accessible to the common man."

Lachlan accepted the book then bowed deeply. "I accept this with much gratitude, Your Grace."

When the king turned to Elizabeth, she curtsied. "Thank you for the gift, Your Grace." She straightened and forced herself to meet his gaze. "You and the queen have been very kind to me over the last three weeks. I apologize if my words hurt you. They were not truly directed at you, but at my own fate."

The king nodded brusquely. "Go with your husband, and for once in your life try to be more than your name. Make your king and country proud of the Ruthven clan once more."

Elizabeth frowned at the comment but said nothing as the king continued.

"You two are the last, best hope for your two clans."

Elizabeth gaped at the man. "That is entirely unreasonable to put the fate of our clans upon our shoulders."

The king's features darkened. "Would you rather I send my ministers to investigate both of your clans, seeking signs of adoration not to your king, but to Satan? For if my men find anything out of the ordinary, you will all be brought up on charges of witchcraft and processed accordingly." He shifted his gaze to Lachlan. "While I do not question the loyalty of the Douglases, their chosen wives have questionable pasts and family ties. Shall I dig deeper into the Ruthvens' history to see what can be revealed?"

Elizabeth couldn't hold back a gasp. The king could easily follow through on his threat and find the simplest reason for anyone to come under suspicion. Her nerves jangling, she took a step away from the king's malevolence. With her heart pounding in her chest she said, "I'll need my things before I leave."

The king smiled grimly. "Your trunk has been packed

and is already loaded on Lachlan's carriage." At Lachlan's start of surprise, the king added, "I had thought you might be leaving us soon so I had the carriage brought around to the courtyard. It awaits you there."

Lachlan bowed again. "Many thanks to both you and the queen." After those gathered went back to their meal, Lachlan turned to Elizabeth. He bent close to her ear and said, "I do not rut. I am not an animal. When you do join your body with mine, Elizabeth, it will be because you want me to be there. It will be because you cannot do otherwise. There will be a day very soon when your every thought, breath, and heartbeat will be focused on the two of us coming together as one."

The warmth of his breath and his very nearness were doing strange things to her nerves, and still she pushed him away. "Never."

"Be prepared to eat those words, Wife. For you shall before the month is through." Elizabeth's gasp of denial was lost as Lachlan turned her toward the doorway. "Shall we depart?"

As they went, Elizabeth stole a peek at the man beside her. Despite her intense dislike of him, she had to admit he was strikingly handsome in his blue-and-green tartan that showed his muscular physique to perfection: strong shoulders, a broad well-muscled chest, and muscular thighs. There was also an indefinable air of self-assurance about him, as if he knew exactly how to handle the situation they now found themselves in. Whereas, she had absolutely no idea of how to proceed now that they would be on their own.

The late morning sky was clear and the day just starting to warm as the carriage rolled through the gatehouse of Falkland Palace and to the south. "You said it would take us four days to reach Whittingehame Castle?"

"Aye," Lachlan said. "We will travel as far as Kirkcaldy tonight."

"Where will we stay?"

"Another of the king's elite guards, one of his Magnificent Seven, Sir Cameron Sinclair, has agreed to shelter us for the night at Ravenscraig Castle. Have no fear. We'll be among friends."

"Your friends. They are not mine." She meant it as a quip, but the truth stung her tongue. "I shall never have friends again now that my family has tossed me away like a worn shoe into our enemy's hands."

If she had hoped for a measure of sympathy from her new husband, she was sadly disappointed. Lachlan's features were grim as the coach rumbled along and their journey began. "I am only your enemy if you make me such." His words hung between them as they raced along the road. The swaying of the carriage, along with the repetitive sounds of the horses' hooves against the hard-packed earth and the vibration of the wheels, soon had Elizabeth nodding off. She'd had very little sleep last night in anticipation of her wedding. Now that the event was behind her, she had a hard time keeping her eyelids from drooping down.

When next she woke, it was to find the carriage had stopped and the door was open, allowing the warm, early evening air inside. The scent of heather floated on the breeze as she moved to step outside the vehicle. As she emerged, Lachlan looked up from where he was stroking the neck of one of the matched bays while the coachman released the other from the carriage harness. "Have we arrived at Kirkcaldy?"

"Nay," Lachlan replied as he reached out his hand to assist her in stepping down. "We had to stop short of our goal because we broke a shaft on one of the wheels. The coachman assures me he can have it repaired before the morning. In the meanwhile, we will stay at Buckhaven Inn for the night."

She accepted his hand and placed one foot on the coach steps but stopped before stepping down as she gaped in horror at the inn before her. The "inn" he mentioned was no more than a rundown country cottage. The mud and mortar walls lurched drunkenly to the right. The thatched roof rippled like the waves she'd see at the Firth of Forth, and smoke escaped from the chimney overhead, but also through the shuttered windows. "This is where we'll be staying?"

"Aye," Lachlan affirmed. "It doesn't look like much, but they have the best meat pasties in the shire."

Elizabeth jerked her hand from his. "Where will we sleep? On the floor?"

"I assure you, we will have a clean room."

Elizabeth paused. "A room together?"

"Aye. We are newlywed and must keep up appearances. However, as I stated before, there will be nothing between us until you desire such." He extended his hand once more.

She stared down at it, trying to decide what to do. She must have hesitated too long, for he stepped forward and his arm came about her waist. He lifted her off her feet before pulling her against his chest. "You will come with me into the inn. It is your choice whether I carry you inside like a sack of grain, or you maintain your dignity and walk inside on your own two feet." He paused as his determined gaze connected with her angry one. "What is your choice?"

Elizabeth relaxed at the mention of a choice, the tension leaving her body.

Lachlan must have read her response as capitulation for he set her on her feet though he held tight to her hand. "Shall we?"

"Since that is the only option I have," she replied tartly. "But only for one night." Her gaze clashed with his as she stepped toward the sagging door.

Inside the inn the smell of smoke lingered, but Elizabeth had to admit the room, while dilapidated and rundown as the rest of the place, was clean. A cheerful fire glowed in the hearth and the wooden tables nearby had a bright bouquet of wildflowers at the center of each that were comprised of pink, yellow, and red blooms.

The gray-haired innkeeper bowed his head upon their entrance and the innkeeper's wife curtsied before coming to greet them. "Welcome, m'laird, milady. We have our best room awaiting ye. Go abovestairs and tae the right." Her curly red hair had streaks of gray and her face was lined with age. But a friendly smile lit her features as she waved them toward a narrow flight of stairs that rose from the center of the room.

"Thank you, Mistress Broun," Lachlan replied as he accepted a candlestick the woman offered, then guided Elizabeth toward the staircase.

"I'll have my son see tae yer bags shortly and in the meanwhile, I'll send up some mutton pasties, cheese, and apples tae fill yer bellies."

"That would be most appreciated." At Elizabeth's hesitation, Lachlan nudged her from behind, forcing her to climb the stairs.

"Will ye be wanting a bath?" Mistress Broun called from below when they had reached the landing above.

At Lachlan's questioning gaze, Elizabeth replied, "Do not trouble yourself, Mistress. We have all we need for the night. But thank you for your kindness."

Mistress Broun offered the pair another curtsey from below before she disappeared from view. With no other distraction, Elizabeth followed Lachlan inside the first room off to their right. Expecting the worst, she was pleasantly surprised when the candlelight revealed a small but tidy bedchamber. The air was not nearly as smoky as belowstairs, and Mistress Broun had obviously put time and effort into sewing matching bedcurtains and a coverlet. A vase of pink, yellow, and red wildflowers—like those below—stood on the nightstand, adding a touch of cheer.

Lachlan lit the brace of candles near the bedside before turning to face her. "Are things better than you feared?"

Elizabeth wrapped her fingers around the bedpost, putting the shaped column of wood between herself and her new husband. "I admit I was wrong."

Lachlan straightened as a shocked expression came to his face. "I did not know a Ruthven could admit such a thing."

Elizabeth frowned. "Then you know very little about Ruthvens," she said sharply.

He did not respond to her barb. Instead, his features became thoughtful. "Neither of us knows the other very well, do we?"

"Nay," she admitted. In the pale wash of the candlelight he looked sincere, but could she trust him? She'd always been told as a Douglas, Lachlan was a barbaric, primitive rogue who was only capable of deception, cheating, and murder. And even though he had not revealed those sides of himself to her yet, he could at any time.

Perhaps this whole thing was an elaborate scheme concocted by him to be rid of her on this, their wedding night. Had he lied about their carriage breaking down and brought her here to this remote and isolated inn under false pretenses so he could kill her in her sleep, then dispose of her body before they ever reached his home?

Lachlan frowned. "Why are you looking at me in that manner?"

"I'm trying to figure out if everything I've ever been told about the Douglases is true."

"And what have you been told? I'm sure it is nothing but lies."

Her gaze narrowed. "Then you can say the Douglases didn't murder Harlan and Helen Ruthven thirty years ago while they slept in their beds, starting this whole feud? Or that a few years later they didn't steal our sheep, killing several clan members who went without food that winter?" While she listed off a few of the offenses committed by his clan she'd been told about, his face turned stony.

"And you can say with a clear conscience that the Ruthvens did not kidnap and impregnate Rosie Douglas? Then, when she was about to give birth, stab her twenty-six times and leave her for dead? When the Douglases found her, she told of the nights of endless abuse by your clansmen. Both she and the baby died."

He came closer and her heart pounded wildly as the room suddenly seemed too small to hold them both. Elizabeth was too frightened to gasp, too frightened to speak, too frightened to do anything but hide behind the sliver of wood separating the two of them.

"Or how about when the Ruthvens poisoned our well,

killing several clansmen before they determined what the cause of the illness was. Do you deny these accusations?"

She swallowed hard, but said nothing.

"Answer me."

She moistened her lips with her tongue. "I only know what I've been told. There is no proof of anything."

"I am proof." Lachlan's voice was fierce. "Your clan robbed me of my parents and the childhood I longed for. And while I was lucky to have cousins whose parents took me in, it doesn't change the fact that your clan took my parents' lives. The Ruthvens are the murders."

He stared at her a long moment and she could feel the hair on the back of her neck raise. Finally, he said, "This is getting us nowhere."

Elizabeth felt a surge of relief. "I am tired. I wish to go to bed."

"What about supper?"

"I'm not hungry."

"All right. I will take some food belowstairs while you prepare yourself for bed. I will join you soon."

Elizabeth stiffened. "In the bed? You said—"

"Take the bed. I will sleep on the floor." Anger and frustration emanated from him in waves that renewed her fear. A heartbeat later, he slipped from the chamber, leaving her alone.

She might not have been able to stop her marriage to this man, but she had to find a way to get away from him before he murdered her in her sleep. Quickly, she scanned the room. There was nothing she could use as a weapon to either attack or defend herself. Could she slip away from him during the night? But where would she go? Could she make her way back to Falkland Palace? Or would there be too many questions asked of her if she did? Could she find her way back to her home even though she had no real notion of where she presently was?

Lachlan had said they were close to Kirkcaldy, which she knew was to the southwest, but could she find her way there alone on a horse she would have to steal? Stealing a horse, even from her husband, was an offense punishable by death.

Elizabeth frowned. She was left with only one option. She had to kill her husband before he killed her.

CHAPTER TWO

THE CANDLE HAD long since burnt down and a hazy gray darkness filled the bedchamber. Elizabeth's hands were shaking as she bent over her husband's sleeping form. Lachlan slept in his kilt and boots on the floor in front of the door. She tensed when she heard his even breathing falter. Did he sense her presence near him?

A moment later, his slow, even breathing resumed and she released a hitched breath. He was still asleep. Silently, she reached for the *sgian-dubh* he kept tucked into his boot. She would have only a second to grab the weapon and strike. Her aim for his throat must be true despite the fact she'd never taken a life before.

There was no other choice. She had to do this. This man was her enemy. She reached for the *sgian-dubh*.

"Touch that and you'll wish *you* were dead." Lachlan's hand snaked around her wrist before she had even touched the weapon.

Elizabeth's blood ran cold. She tried to wrench away, but he was too strong. "Let me go."

"Why?" He held tight as he sat up, watching her with an

intensity that made her stomach tighten. "So you can try again to kill me with my own weapon?"

Her blood pounded in her ears. "It's not what you think."

"It's not?" He stood, pulling her up with him. Pain shot through her wrist at the motion. "'Tis obvious to me that you intended to slit my throat. I thought we had moved past all this."

"You were planning to kill me, so I thought I'd kill you first."

He stared at her in stunned amazement. "You thought I would kill you? Whatever gave you that idea?"

"How could you not? We are who we are. How can our marriage change anything?" she replied, starting to feel a little light-headed as she locked her knees to keep herself upright.

He turned her in his arms until they fully faced each other. She drew a breath.

As he loosened his grip, he gazed down at her. "Why would I hurt you? You are my wife."

She stepped back, suddenly noticing the darkness of the bedchamber had given way to the pinkish light of dawn. "We stopped for the night in the middle of nowhere. It would be easy for you to murder me here and hide my body where no one would ever find it."

Lachlan frowned. "We were forced to stop here because of the wheel. There was nothing sinister in my motives, I assure you. But we cannot continue our journey with this distrust between us."

Lachlan bent down and withdrew his *sgian-dubh* from his boot, then he reached for the Bible the king and queen had given them as a gift.

"What are you doing?" Her voice sounded frightened even to her own ears.

He set the Bible on the bed beside them, then with his weapon in his right hand he pierced the palm of his left hand, drawing a thin trickle of blood. "Now give me your left hand."

She stepped farther away. "I don't understand."

"I'll not live all my days with dread of each other. Swear to God you'll not kill me or cause my death and I will swear the same to you."

When she didn't respond, he stood there, waiting until finally she offered her hand. He held her gently as the knife's edge bit into her flesh and the warmth of her own blood trailed across her palm.

"Take my left hand in yours and place your other hand atop mine on this Bible."

She'd always been told the Douglases were oath-breakers, yet he wanted to place their hands on a Bible and as such she could honestly believe that he meant to keep this one promise to her. She drew a long breath, then settled her right hand over his and extended her left hand toward him. He wrapped his larger fingers around her smaller ones. The warmth of his blood merged with her own.

In the intimate silence he said, "I, Lachlan, solemnly swear never to harm you, Elizabeth. I will protect you and keep you all the days of my life."

As though compelled by a force outside of herself, Elizabeth replied, "I, Elizabeth, solemnly swear never to harm you. I will honor you and keep you all the days of my life." As soon as she said the words, a strange warmth moved through her. The pledge they offered each other somehow seemed far more binding and intimate than the marriage vows they had said only yesterday.

"Our blood oath is unbreakable. It was not given as a Douglas to a Ruthven, but as a man to a woman. Are we agreed?"

"Aye. And you agree?"

"Aye," he echoed. "We shall both bear a scar on our palms to remind us of our promise."

His voice was hoarse, but she thought she heard something in his tone—respect, perhaps, or even admiration. She held on to his hand a moment longer, then slipped her fingers from his and reached for the cloth atop the washstand next to the basin and pitcher. She ripped the cloth lengthwise to create two small strips before dipping the remainder of the cloth in the water in the basin. She wiped the blood from her hand before taking Lachlan's hand in hers and doing the same.

Once that was complete, she set the remains of the

bloody cloth next to the washbasin and picked up one of the clean strips of linen. She wound it around Lachlan's hand then tied the ends in a knot. She held the second strip out to him, beckoning him without words to do the same for her.

As he tied the knot, the crowing of a rooster in the yard below heralded the arrival of dawn. "How do we proceed from here?" Elizabeth asked.

"We do exactly that. We proceed on our journey." His lips pulled up at the corners as he gazed down at his bandaged hand.

A flutter came to her stomach that had nothing to do with hunger. He appeared pleased with this new commitment between them. Was she? A moment later, her stomach grumbled loudly. Perhaps it was her hunger speaking after all and not her nerves.

A concerned look came to Lachlan's face at the odd sound. "When was the last time you ate something?"

"I had a small amount at our wedding breakfast, but nothing since," she admitted as her stomach growled again.

"Why don't you dress and pack your things. I will go find us some food," he said, then left her alone in the bedchamber.

Elizabeth moved to the bed. Struggling for control, she balanced carefully on the edge of the mattress, listening to the soft nickering of a horse followed by the crowing of a rooster in the yard below. She glanced down at her bandaged hand. What had she done? She had willingly agreed not to harm her enemy. And if she went back on her part of the oath, she would be without honor, which was worse than betraying her clan.

It was well enough, she told herself. She could honor the oath and still keep herself apart from Lachlan Douglas. She had agreed not to kill him, but that didn't make her his friend. She clenched her teeth, staring stonily into the growing light of the morning.

Even though she was surrounded by light, a dark loneliness settled inside her as it had so many times before. She would be alone in this new life of hers just as she had been alone even among her own clan. Yet, as always, she would make the best of the situation. She'd learned long ago not to rely on others for her happiness. In the past, that had only ended in disappointment. She would make the best of her new life in the days, months, and years ahead.

"I'll shape a future," she said, trying to convince herself. Elizabeth took a deep breath and slowly released it. Perhaps if she said the words often enough, she might actually start to believe them.

IN THE COMMON room belowstairs Lachlan found Mistress Broun with her head resting on one of the wooden tables. Her eyes were open, but she gazed off into the distance as though seeing into the otherworld. He stopped beside her and placed a gentle hand on her shoulder. Heat radiated from beneath his hand. She was feverish. "Mistress? Are you well?"

Slowly the older woman lifted her head and turned her glassy gaze on him. Her body wavered and her eyes were large, her pupils dilated in the gauntness of her face.

"You should be in bed, my good woman. Where is your husband? Do you have any maids who can see you to your bed?" The woman was definitely ill. He had seen that same look in others' eyes when they had been in the thrall of a fever for several hours. Lachlan straightened, thinking back to when not long ago he had helped his cousin Vivian heal those who were ill at Redhouse Castle. The herbalist had given her patients some kind of potion—what herbs had it contained? He recalled something about elderflowers and peppermint.

Instead of standing over the innkeeper's wife, Lachlan sat down, gazing more directly at the woman. She stared at him, and despite her fever, he suddenly felt as though she saw every vulnerable part of him—the part that was not quite equal to his famous cousins, the part that feared being abandoned, the part that hated feeling a loss of control. An overwhelming urge to turn away from her knowing eyes came over him, but he resisted, falling back into anger instead.

"Clearly something is wrong, Mistress. What would you have me do?"

Something flickered in her eyes. "Ale. If you would be so kind." Her fingers were white where they grasped the corner of the table as she tried to remain upright.

Instantly, Lachlan regretted his outburst as he stood and turned to grab a pitcher of ale and a mug from the table behind them. He poured a mugful and offered it to the woman.

She drained the mug, then collapsed against the table, sending the pewter vessel to the floor with a clang. At the noise, a young maid hastened into the chamber.

"Mistress?" the blonde-haired girl stopped short at the sight of Lachlan. She was no more than thirteen or possibly fourteen years of age. "Beg pardon, m'laird." She turned around and made to leave again.

"Nay. Do not go, please. I need your help."

The girl came forward again. The fear vanished from her expression as she offered him a hesitant smile.

"How long has Mistress Broun been like this?" Lachlan asked.

"I dinna ken. I've just now arrived. I heard a noise and came runnin'."

"Can you tell me where she sleeps?"

The maid nodded. "There's a bed in the back where she and the master sleep."

Lachlan lifted the feverish woman into his arms. "Show me."

The maid led him to the back of the inn where a curtain

hung, separating the bedchamber from the common room. Lachlan pushed the fabric aside and entered the darkened space. He set the innkeeper's wife on the bed, propping her head up with pillows, then turned to the girl. "Can you take me to your kitchen?"

Her face was shadowed but he could see the slightest bob of her head. He followed her down a hallway until they came to a doorway on the right. She stopped outside. "My sister, Meg, helps the mistress cook."

Lachlan entered the room to find a slightly taller blonde-haired girl who was only a few years older than her sister. She stirred a pot of porridge, and tended a pan of blood sausage on a grate over the flames. The beginnings of the morning fare for the inn, no doubt. "Good morrow," Lachlan greeted when the girl looked from him to her sister and back again.

Her eyes went wide. "Jane, ye know the mistress hates it when ye bring visitors into her kitchen."

"Do not blame your sister," Lachlan said, coming forward. "I asked her to bring me here. Your mistress is in the grip of a fever. I came to see if you might have some dried elderflowers and peppermint that I can make into a tisane."

The girl's features became troubled—from his request or the news that her mistress was ill, he was not certain. "Ye ken about herbs?"

"Not myself, nay, but my cousin-in-law is quite knowledgeable and I have watched her use that combination many times to ease a fever."

"What if mistress dies from the brew?" Meg asked hesitantly.

"The herbs are harmless enough. I assure you she will not die if you help me quickly. Where are those herbs?"

She must have sensed his growing frustration because she moved quickly to a shelf on the opposite side of the room and took down two clay jars, which she handed to him. "These are what you need."

To the younger woman who still hovered near the door he said, "Will you help me get some boiling water so your sister can return to her duties for the inn?"

With a look of relief, Meg returned to her cooking and Jane hastened to the hearth. After wrapping the handle in a cloth, she retrieved the kettle hanging on a hook above the flames. She brought the boiling water to him along with a bowl. "Will ye teach me how tae brew the herbs?"

"Are you interested in healing?" Lachlan asked as he measured out equal parts of both the elderflower and peppermint, adding them to the bowl.

Jane nodded. "It has always been of interest tae me."

Lachlan showed her how Vivian had taught him to steep the herbs and strain them. They poured some of the golden liquid into a mug for Mistress Broun. "If you are truly interested in studying the art of healing, I can write to my cousin when I am home and ask her if she would consider taking you on as an apprentice."

Her eyes flew wide. "Ye would do that fer me?"

"If that is what you wish, then, aye."

"I wish it with all my heart." The girl was all smiles as they left the kitchen and returned to the ailing woman's bedside. Lachlan set the candlestick he carried next to the bedside, casting her face in mottled shades of gray. Mistress Broun's eyes were closed and her breathing shallow. "Where is her husband?"

"He always hunts at this time in the mornin'. Whatever he catches becomes the special meal fer the day."

"I hope he returns soon," Lachlan said as he helped to prop the sleepy woman up on her pillows, then instructed Jane how to spoon the cooling liquid into the older woman's mouth.

"How will we know if it worked?" Jane looked questioningly at him.

Lachlan shrugged. "I'm no healer. I only imitated what I saw a real healer do, but I imagine she will be better when her fever breaks and her skin resumes its normal pink tone instead of her current gray pallor."

Jane warily placed the back of her fingers against Mistress Broun's forehead. "She feels less warm to the touch and she looks better to me already."

Lachlan studied the woman's unresponsive face. "I suppose she does."

"What are you doing?" a female voice interrupted.

Lachlan lifted his gaze to see Elizabeth standing inside the curtain, assessing both him and Jane. He inhaled sharply, clenching his hands into fists at his sides. There was something different about the way she was looking at him. No longer was her gaze filled with antagonism and annoyance. Instead, there was a catlike watchfulness, as though she were trying to determine something about him, or was it the beginning of a connection between them? "The innkeeper's wife took ill."

"I thought you were in a hurry to leave this place?"

Annoyance flared, forcing any connection he might have imagined away. "The woman was alone in the common room. She was helpless. I felt it was my duty to assist her."

Elizabeth's face clouded. "You seem to be very good at helping women in distress."

He held Elizabeth's gaze for a few heartbeats while he tried to discern if she was being sarcastic or serious. Uncertain, he turned to Jane. "I shall leave this good woman in your care since my wife and I must now depart."

Jane offered him a hesitant smile. "I'll do what I can tae help her."

"And I will write to my cousin on your behalf."

"Thank you, m'laird."

He held the curtain aside for Elizabeth to pass through before joining her on the other side. "Come with me to the kitchen. We can break our fast, then be on our way if the wheel is fixed."

"Can we not depart immediately?"

He turned and looked at her in surprise. "Abovestairs

you said you were hungry. Famished even."

She clasped her hands around her upper arms. A slight shiver moved through her. "I'd rather we be on our way."

"You are a very confusing woman." He blew out a soft, frustrated breath. "I must insist we at least stop by the kitchen and gather a few things we can eat on our way. Will that be acceptable?"

She looked away but not before he saw a shadow of fear in her eyes. "If you must."

"What is wrong, Elizabeth? I know we do not know each other well yet, but you can trust me."

"Will you trust me as well?"

He gave her a soft smile. "That's usually how this works. I trust you. You trust me."

"Then I need you to trust me now and promise not to ask why when I suggest a change to our travel plans."

He hesitated. What was she up to? Finally, he nodded. "I am not unreasonable. What do you suggest?"

"Instead of heading southwest to Kirkcaldy and Ravenscraig Castle, would you head due west for several miles and then turn to the south?"

The question as to why burned upon his tongue, but he clenched his teeth to keep himself from asking it. He'd told her he trusted her. Now was the time to prove that. He nodded. "If that is what you wish, then that will be the route we take."

ELIZABETH HUGGED HERSELF all the harder, trying to still the trembling of her hands. Lachlan had agreed with her plan without question. She had not expected that. Yet he once again disproved what she'd been told about him her whole life: that the entire Douglas clan was unreasonable, diabolical, and cruel.

Instead, in the time she had known Lachlan Douglas in particular, he had talked her out of taking her own life, had vowed to her father to keep her safe, and hadn't retaliated against her for trying to slit his throat. Leaving her to wonder yet again what truth to believe about him and his clan. Was Lachlan a saint, a sinner, or somewhere in between?

She took a deep breath to steady her nerves as she and Lachlan headed for the kitchen. How could she determine for herself exactly who the man she had married was? Would more time together reveal his true self? Should she stay with him and find out or leave right now?

Her clan could extract her from her current circumstances this very morning if she wanted them to. After Lachlan had left their bedchamber, she'd pushed the shutters back in order to breathe the morning air with the hopes it would clear her head. Instead of clearing her thoughts, they became conflicted when she saw a small army had made camp in the distance, appearing like a blight on the gently sloping hills. Smoke from their campfires came to her like a specter, and the wind carried their voices through the silence of the dawn.

Elizabeth was convinced it was her father and his men. The thought should have filled her with joy, and yet fear filled her instead. The fresh cut on her palm stung as she remembered her vow to keep Lachlan safe from harm. Which is why she had asked him to change his plans for their travel. Her clan would expect them to take the shortest path along the coast. They would never expect Lachlan to head in the opposite direction, adding miles to their journey.

Because of her suggestion, both she and Lachlan would be safe for a few hours at least, until her father figured out their deception and pursued them once more. Perhaps in that time she could finally determine what to believe about the man she had married. Was he her nemesis or something else entirely? And if she decided he might not be what she'd always been told, she would have to ask him to trust her once more when she asked him to leave the carriage behind and travel on horseback to escape her own clan's deadly plans. For she knew her father would kill Lachlan if they caught up to them. Then the Douglases would retaliate, and the feud would continue even though the king had demanded they put an end to it all.

With a sigh of frustration that she and Lachlan were stuck in the middle of the strife between the two clans, Elizabeth remained at the kitchen doorway while Lachlan negotiated with the young woman about breakfast fare that would travel well. He stood near the hearth, his big body cast in hues of red and gold by the flames. His blond hair held a slight wave that brushed the nape of his neck, and a few errant curls caressed his brow and temples. Despite the fact he had slept in his clothing from the day before, his snowy-white shirt still looked pristine as did the blue and green fabric of his kilt.

Even in their less than perfect circumstances, he appeared refined and elegant. With a soft brogue in his voice, he spoke to the young women with both authority and respect. He certainly did not give the impression of someone who was overbearing and ruthless. Or was all this an act to lull her into his web?

With a start she realized his blue eyes were upon her. He was frowning slightly, no doubt curious to know why she scrutinized him so. Instead of giving in to the desire to look away, she continued to hold his gaze. *Who are you, Lachlan Douglas? What will I gain by remaining your wife?*

CHAPTER THREE

THE SKY TURNED a purplish gray as the sun's rays sank below the horizon. Even in the hazy light, Elizabeth could see the road they followed skirted the banks of the Firth of Forth, until suddenly they turned and started to make their way up a long, winding road.

The last several hours had been a test not just to her nerves, but also to her endurance as she worried about what lay ahead. Until now she and Lachlan had been alone for the most part. At Ravenscraig Castle, they would be surrounded by many—so many whom she did not know. What kind of reception would she receive at the home of his friend? Would the residents there stare at her and sneer contemptuously just like her kin always did when they spoke of the Douglases?

They continued climbing the road ahead for what seemed like forever until suddenly the castle brose before them, rising from the sheer edge of a bluff. The gray-colored stones stood tall and stark against the dying shades of twilight. The castle had twin round towers joined by saw-toothed battlements. Ravenscraig was not simply a castle. It was a fortress.

The closer they came, the faster her heart beat in her chest. They passed through the gatehouse, beneath the portcullis, and across a planked bridge before entering the main castle. Its entrance was marked by a torch on either side of double black doors that were opened wide in greeting. As the carriage came to a stop, Elizabeth could hear the murmur of excited voices from beyond the vehicle. When the carriage door opened, she saw several men and women rushing out the castle's main entrance to greet their guests.

Elizabeth straightened. "It appears we have arrived."

Lachlan looked at her for the first time in hours. "And now that we are here, I need a promise from you."

She regarded him coldly. "We already promised to do no harm to each other through the oath we took this morning. What more do you want from me?"

His jaw tightened. He shifted his gaze from her to the men—draped in tartan cloth dyed in red, green, and blue—who gathered outside the carriage door. Some carried torches, others lanterns, casting the courtyard in both bright yellow-gold light and deep shadow. "I want your promise that you'll not show if you've taken offense to anything that is said here. These people are my friends, and as such, they know my history. Some of them were with me after the death of my parents. Others have grown to hate the Ruthvens because of their many crimes against the king and this country."

He turned to face her once again, his blue eyes picking

up the shimmering light of the lanterns. "I will see you are safe."

The silence between them grew until she was certain he could hear the frantic beating of her heart. She had no idea her clan was loathed by so many in Scotland. "Hate? Crimes?"

Lachlan frowned. "Aye. They are often reviled."

There was something in his simple claim that rocked her. He made her hear a veracity in the words. There had been times she'd wondered when she'd heard whispered conversations that stopped the moment she appeared, and situations that didn't quite align with what she'd been told . . .

Her father and her clan had kept her sheltered from the outside world all her life. Everything she knew about the world came from the stories her father or other members of the clan recounted for her. Her perspective about society and the way the world worked had come to her not from her own experience, but filtered through others. Had they told her the truth?

Elizabeth crossed her arms over her chest in a futile attempt to comfort herself. Even while she'd waited at the palace for her wedding to Lachlan, she'd started to notice a different perspective. Her father had always told her the king adored the Ruthven clan and granted them the highest of privileges within his court. But what she'd observed was that even though two of the queen's ladies-in-waiting were Ruthvens, the king did not approve of them attending his wife. He wanted them gone from the palace and his life. That truth aligned with what Lachlan had told her just now.

At her hesitation, Lachlan frowned. "'Tis but a simple aye or nay, Elizabeth. What is it to be? Will you promise not to react to any perceived slights?"

What was the truth and what was a lie? Though her thoughts still spun, she said, "I promise."

At her agreement, Lachlan took her hand in his and helped her from the carriage. Immediately upon their descent, they were engulfed by those gathered. The men offered Lachlan handshakes and claps upon the back, while the women hugged him with smiles and laughter. One woman with red hair tugged him farther into the crowd and toward the entrance of the castle, forcing Elizabeth to release Lachlan's hand until she stood alone outside the gathered group.

He kept looking back at her with an apology in his eyes.

She straightened and clasped her hands together, refusing to let anyone see how alone she felt.

At the entrance, a tall, elegant man stood patiently, bathed in the light that spilled from within the castle. The light revealed a face of stunning comeliness. Every feature on his face came close to perfection and his body brimmed with strength. He wore tan breeches and a dark surcoat with a pristine white shirt beneath. Without even an introduction, Elizabeth surmised this was Cameron Sinclair, the laird of Ravenscraig Castle. Lachlan approached him.

Slowly the gathered crowd grew silent and turned, watching the reunion of the two men.

"We were prepared for your arrival yesterday," Cameron Sinclair said.

"Our late arrival couldn't be helped. We had a bit of misfortune on the road," Lachlan replied as he stood before his friend and struck his chest with his fist once in salute before they came together in a sudden embrace. It triggered an eruption of cheers from those gathered. The red-haired woman once again clutched Lachlan's arm, keeping him by her side.

"Well, you're here now," Cameron said over a swelling of whispers from those gathered as their eyes turned to Elizabeth, who yet stood alone.

A chill came over her when she saw she was forgotten no longer as she remained by the carriage where he had left her. The expressions of those gathered ranged from curious to hostile. And the red-haired woman's lips pulled up in a satisfied smile.

"It is good to see you, Mariam, but you must excuse me." Lachlan released himself from the red-haired woman's clutches and walked back to Elizabeth's side, offering her his arm. He cast her a smile before guiding her back toward Cameron Sinclair himself. Around them the crowd had fallen silent. "Cameron, may I present to you my wife, Elizabeth." He turned to her and said, "This is Sir Cameron Sinclair."

Elizabeth was all too aware of everyone staring at her. The red-haired woman glared. Ignoring her, Elizabeth looked to the other ladies who were all so regal and elegant, with nary a hair out of place, while she was certain she looked like a wild banshee with her brown hair mussed from their travels. Regardless of her appearance, she curtsied, then straightened, waiting to see along with the others how the laird would respond to a Ruthven in their midst.

The dark-haired laird studied her intently. He seemed to sense her fear as he took one of her icy hands in his own and lifted it to his lips. The soft salute was followed by a smile. "You are welcome, Elizabeth. Here you will only be known for who you are now, not who you have been," Cameron said.

Elizabeth's cheeks flamed at yet another piece of evidence that her family and their reputation were not as stellar as she'd been taught. Until she learned the truth for herself, she would keep silent. "Thank you, my laird. That is very gracious of you."

Cameron looked down at her with compassion in his eyes. "Everyone deserves a second chance. Consider this yours. Lachlan is a good man. He deserves a devoted and loving wife."

At his words, Elizabeth's gaze slid to Lachlan's. She was neither of those things at the moment. And perhaps she never would be. She had no time to think further on the matter when Lachlan slipped his arm around her waist and urged her forward into the castle and away from the crowd. "Come, let us clean up from our travels, then rest before supper. We have another long day ahead of us on the morrow."

Elizabeth allowed herself to be ushered forward. Her body felt heavy and her mind weary beyond words. Her troubles would still be with her in the morning, but mayhap after a bath, a meal, and a night's sleep she would be better able to face them.

Inside the castle, Cameron led them along a richly paneled hallway hung with tapestries and portraits of centuries of Sinclair family history. Lachlan and Cameron chatted along the way, but she paid no mind to their conversation as they passed several rooms—a library, a receiving room, a solar, the great hall. At the end of the long hallway they climbed a set of stairs and continued down another hallway until they stopped outside the open door of a large bedchamber. "Your room," Cameron said.

As they stepped in, Lachlan turned to her and for a heartbeat she forgot to breathe. The setting sun filtered through the arched window of the bedchamber, giving the large room a strange, yellowish glow. She watched as the light limned her husband's hair, making it nearly gold where the unruly locks curled against his temple.

A similar light flared in his eyes. She'd seen that look in the eyes of other men before, and it had always unsettled her, but in this instance, she felt an even greater panic. They would spend yet another night alone together. And this time she wouldn't be thinking murderous thoughts. If she wasn't thinking of murder, then what would she be thinking about? Her mouth went dry as she tried not to look at him.

"I'll have a tub sent up so you can clean yourselves before our evening meal," Cameron said with a bow, and closing the room's door, leaving them to themselves. At the sudden thought of being alone with her husband while he bathed, Elizabeth clasped her arms tightly around herself, hugging her suddenly shivering body.

Lachlan did not miss her response. His smile turned stiff. "Why are you still afraid of me? I've vowed not to harm you." Something flickered in his eyes. "I am a man of my word, Elizabeth."

"And why should I trust you? I am surrounded by strangers. I have no idea who I can trust except myself."

"I've assured you that you are safe. Now stop this non-sense and get yourself ready for first your bath and then supper."

Elizabeth backed up a step. "It was obvious upon our arrival that just as you said . . . they all hate me—a Ruthven. I have no intention of subjecting myself to more of their hostility by attending a supper tonight."

Lachlan's featured darkened. "You are my wife, and as such I insist you accompany me. I will make certain no one abuses you in any way." His expression softened. "I'm sure you will feel better once you've had something to eat."

She squared her shoulders. "I'm not hungry. Besides, I do not feel well enough to eat."

His brow arched. "Well then, if you are ill, it is my husbandly duty to remain here with you and see that you sustain no further hardship."

"After a bath, I plan to go to bed."

A gleam came into his eyes. "I would be delighted to join you."

"You are a swine." She frowned. "I am not so feverish that I'd think to want to bed you."

He folded his arms over his chest, his features growing darker once more. "Then you'll come to supper with me."

"You cannot force me."

He took a step toward her. "Is that a challenge I hear, my dear wife?"

"If you touch me, I'll scream."

He shrugged. "Do so. As you so elegantly pointed out, we are surrounded by people who know me far better than they know you."

Elizabeth felt the blood drain from her face. "You are not a swine. You are the Devil himself."

Lachlan grabbed her and wrenched her forward into a crushing embrace. "If that is what you wish me to be, then so be it. I was trying to give you time to adjust to your new position as my wife. But if you will only think of me as a beast or worse, then perhaps I should become just that and take what is rightfully mine."

She had no time to protest as his mouth claimed hers. His lips were hot and possessive. He gave her only a heartbeat to adjust before he demanded more, probing her lips with his tongue until, on a gasp, she let him in.

He plunged and stroked, sending mindless reverberations through her limbs. Her knees quivered and threatened to give way as his hand came up to twist in the length of her hair, ensuring she could not pull away or avoid his relentless plundering. His other hand moved to the back of her gown and fumbled with the lacings, loosening them enough that he slid his hand inside the fabric of her gown and above her chemise. Her smothered cry was ignored as he splayed his hand against the thin cotton that did little to protect her from his velvet touch.

Her protest became a groan as his roving fingers sent waves of sensation across her flesh. This time her knees did give way, but he held her up, deepening his kiss, teasing her flesh until she could scarcely breathe, scarcely think as waves and waves of glorious delight rippled through her.

He pulled back, but not away. "Shall we stop playing games, Elizabeth? I want this. You want this. Forget who we are and just give in to what you feel." His lips traced a trail of fire from her lips to the slender arch of her throat and back again.

"Nay," she gasped. "I cannot take anything from you." Her mind was fighting the pleasure but her body reveled in his possession as he traced a line of kisses across her chin and neck. She shuddered with raw desire as his lips trailed across her hungry flesh. Everywhere he touched, she burned and longed for more, never knowing, never dreaming such intimacy was possible with a man she should despise.

She'd said she wasn't hungry, but that was a lie. She was suddenly starving for more of what Lachlan offered her as his lips stroked the flesh above her bodice. A soft groan filled the air. She startled when she realized it came from her own throat. Her eyes fluttered open to find him staring down at her, studying her with an intense stillness as his heart thundered in his chest. She could see in the blue depths of his eyes that he wanted her, that he was fighting his own hunger every bit as much as she wanted to fight her own. That fact should have frightened her, but it did not. Instead, it made her smile.

She'd thought she was weaponless against Lachlan, but she was not. A kiss could render him more vulnerable than any dagger ever could. Testing her theory, she brought her hand up to his cheek. Instantly, he pressed into her touch as a shudder racked his body.

Lachlan Douglas might be a warrior and her enemy, but she had power over him. He would be lost to her touch anytime she chose to wield her new weapon.

As though sensing the direction of her thoughts, he grasped her hand and pulled it away from his cheek. Every muscle in his body tense, he took a measured step back. "Accompany me to supper this evening."

Knowing she had no other choice, Elizabeth nodded. "You really are a loathsome creature, you know."

Lachlan stared at her for a long moment. "Only you can change the way you see others, Elizabeth. They will be exactly what you want them to be. Consider that while you bathe."

"You're not staying?"

His hands clenched at his sides. "Take the tub for yourself. I will bathe with the men in the barracks. I shall see you at supper." With a bow of his head, he left.

She felt suddenly cold, and an unfamiliar pain settled in her stomach as she turned away from the door. For a long while, she stared at the bed in the center of the chamber, not seeing the golden bedcover or fine silk drapes that surrounded the bed, but the unknown emotion in a pair of blue eyes framed by golden lashes. She now had a new weapon to use against him. But using it would come with a price—a price that would reduce her to little more than what she'd claimed him to be: the most loathsome of creatures.

LACHLAN STRODE WITH angry footsteps down the hallway. His blood still pounded in his veins as the scent of Elizabeth lingered on his skin. He'd come close to simply throwing her on the bed and getting her out of his system.

Was that the answer? Would physically possessing her

body finally ease the frustration he felt every time they were in close proximity to each other? Or would such an act only make matters worse? He wanted her to come to him willingly, and he was prepared to wait for such a moment, but just when he thought he had himself under control, she would bait him with her words—cut him as deeply as any edged weapon might.

He released a growl of frustration.

"Trouble already?"

Lachlan paused, as his gaze connected with his host's. Cameron Sinclair arched his brows as he leaned against the doorjamb of a chamber farther down the hallway. "Nothing I cannot handle."

Cameron angled his head inside the chamber. "Come, indulge in a dram of whisky. You look downright miserable for a man who is so newly wed."

Lachlan sighed and raked a hand through his hair. "It shows?"

"Aye." Cameron headed toward a table positioned between two chairs that held a full bottle of whisky. He poured two glasses and handed one to Lachlan. "What are you going to do about your pretty little wife?"

He took the offered glass and sank into one of the chairs. "I wasn't aware I needed to do anything about her." Silence stretched between them until Lachlan finally added, "You don't understand."

Cameron sat opposite him. His dark eyes narrowed.

"You're right. I don't understand."

"She is my wife."

"She's certainly not taking up that role with any serious-ness or you would be in the bedchamber with her now."

"She feels unwanted and threatened."

"By you?"

"Nay," Lachlan said, unable to keep the cold edge from his voice. "Perhaps. It would help if everyone stopped looking at Elizabeth as though she were the enemy."

Cameron's features darkened. "The Ruthvens started this whole feud thirty years ago when they kidnapped, abused, then murdered Rosie Douglas. It's been a constant battle since then with the Douglases striking back followed by a Ruthven retaliation until fourteen years ago they murdered your parents. Ruthvens *have* been our enemy—the Sinclairs and the Douglases alike. How can your marriage to one slip of a girl change all that?"

"Elizabeth wasn't involved in any of that personally." Lachlan hesitated for a moment, then pushed his anger aside. "I cannot change the past. However, I can change the course of my future with Elizabeth. Not as enemies but as some-thing more."

"Judging by what I saw of the girl, that is a battle you might not win," Cameron said, then finished the contents of his glass in one final gulp.

Lachlan's anger flared as he set his glass aside. "I would not be a Douglas if I didn't at least try."

Cameron's lips pulled up in a half grin. "You are becoming more like your cousins Reid and Quinn every day."

Lachlan suddenly frowned. "I shall take that as a compliment."

"'Tis how it is meant." Cameron stood. "I've not seen this side of you before, my friend. You are becoming your own man, following your own counsel instead of staying in the shadows cast by your more famous cousins."

Lachlan stood, matching Cameron's gaze with his own steady one. "I am more determined than ever to move beyond the past."

"I hope she is worthy of you."

As Lachlan's anger ebbed, a tiny bud of hope unfolded within. "Elizabeth is definitely spirited. Life with her will never be predictable. You said you were willing to give her a second chance, despite her name. And if that doesn't work, perhaps you could give her a third as well."

Cameron angled his head as he grinned. "I cannot decide if you are the most optimistic man I've even known, or a fool."

Lachlan shrugged. "Perhaps both. Time will reveal all, I suppose."

Cameron reached for the whisky bottle once more and poured a splash into both their glasses before handing Lachlan's back to him. "Here's to whatever your future brings." Cameron lifted his own glass in salute. "*Slàinte mhath.*"

Lachlan joined his friend in a toast. "Good health to you as well."

When their glasses were empty, Cameron said, "Since it appears you are not welcome in your own chamber at the moment, should I have a bath brought up for you here?"

"Nay," Lachlan replied. "I had intended to bathe in the barracks."

Cameron shook his head. "What kind of host would I be if I allowed that? I insist you clean up here."

Lachlan nodded his gratitude. "Thank you, my friend."

"No thanks are necessary. But just be forewarned, I do intend to keep an eye on your . . . what did you call her? Your unpredictable wife."

Lachlan released his breath in a rush. "That makes two of us."

CHAPTER FOUR

AFTER ELIZABETH HAD bathed and changed her clothing, she stood by the fire drying her hair. As she combed her fingers through the damp tendrils, she stared at her reflection in the looking glass, not liking what she saw. She couldn't help but compare herself to the women belowstairs who seemed so refined, serene, and in control. Whereas her own face was pale and strained. Dark shadows appeared beneath her eyes from a lack of sleep over the past week. She did not recognize the woman looking back at her.

When did I turn into a stranger to myself? She'd done so many things in the past few days she wasn't proud of. She'd almost taken her own life, had attempted to slit her husband's throat, and her snappish behavior toward Lachlan was entirely out of character. A wave of self-loathing washed through her and she closed her eyes, fighting it. Her whole life had become a tumultuous mess. She didn't know who she could trust or what to believe. Had her father and her clan told her the truth about their activities or their reputation? Or were the Douglases controlling the narrative by placing her in situations and around people supportive to them? Or did any of that really matter?

For the first time in her life she was free from the constraints of her clan. She could judge for herself what was real, what was the truth. She had to stop thinking of herself as a victim in this marriage and start taking charge of her own life, thoughts, and actions. She might be surrounded by strangers, but she was not alone, for she knew without a doubt that Lachlan would not abandon her despite how badly she'd treated him up to this point.

She looked down at her palm. The evidence of their pact had already started to heal. Was it time to at least give Lachlan a chance to prove her clan wrong as well?

When her hair was finally dried, Elizabeth paused. She should restrain her hair in a snood or in a knot at the back of her head as was the custom for married women, but she resisted the urge to do so. Was it because she didn't want to acknowledge the fact that she truly was married? Or was it because she didn't feel married? She frowned as she considered her options. In the end, she opted to place a lace veil over the top of her hair.

When she was done, she straightened. Her anxieties had settled and her fears had been tucked away for now. The ghost of her old self seemed to creep back into her skin as she made her way toward the door. Lachlan had said she was to meet him in the great hall. She knew if she stayed in the chamber much longer, he would no doubt come up to get her.

Without anything else to delay her, Elizabeth left the bedchamber and made her way along the corridor to the stairs. She started to descend then stopped when a movement at the bottom caught her attention. Lachlan stepped from the shadows and into the light.

At the sight of him, her breath caught. He had cleaned up from their travels as well. And while he still wore a length of blue and green tartan that was pleated into a kilt and held in place by a polished leather belt, he also wore a formal coat in a rich shade of midnight blue, the cuffs of which were turned back and trimmed in wide gold braid. The coat was open to reveal a snowy-white shirt beneath with a neck scarf edged in lace. The end of his tartan was brought up over his shoulder and pinned to the coat with a silver brooch in a trinity Celtic knot. His face was shaved clean and his hair curled as it had dried against his temples and at his nape.

For a long moment Elizabeth held her breath as she took in the sight. He was the same man she had traveled here with and yet in this moment he looked so different and powerful—as though he could lift or lower his hand and make the tides rise and fall at will. Despite the change in his appearance, his eyes remained the same. Startling blue eyes studied her as she once again strode forward. She kept her hand on the railing to steady herself until she stood before him at the bottom of the stairs.

"You look lovely," Lachlan said as his eyes drifted over her face, then traveled lower over the swell of her bosom rising above the neckline of her forest-green gown. Did he see the turmoil she had seen in her own face? If he did, he gave no indication as he slipped his hand under her elbow. "Shall we?"

He steered her into the great hall. The roar of conversation came to her as she took comfort in Lachlan's touch. Beneath the glittering candles, splashes of multi-colored tartan could be seen in every corner of the room. As soon as the two of them entered the chamber, all conversation ceased and all eyes turned their way. Heat warmed her as she noted the looks were not ones of welcome. Some looks were leery. Some were outright hostile and followed by whispered responses that left no doubt the anger was directed at her and her alone.

"So it is true. Lachlan Douglas did indeed marry a Ruthven," came a whisper off to her right.

"Even that beautiful dress cannot hide the blackness of her soul," came another whisper from the left.

The woman Lachlan had greeted as Mariam stepped before them. She wore a beautiful rust brocade gown that highlighted the fiery red of her hair. She looked at the two of them for a heartbeat before her gaze narrowed. "A Judas in our very midst. Whatever shall we do with her?"

"That's unfair, Mariam." Lachlan pulled Elizabeth infinitesimally closer. "You do not even know Elizabeth yet. Just as you are more than your clan name, allow my wife the same courtesy." He stepped past Mariam and deftly guided

Elizabeth through the crowd until she saw Cameron Sinclair sitting among several elegantly dressed men and women.

"I hope we did not keep you waiting while we shook off our travel dirt," Lachlan greeted. From somewhere two goblets were thrust into their hands.

Cameron raised the glass he held. "To the newlyweds. Having you here with us now was worth the wait. Here's to a joining of two noble families for the betterment of all of Scotland." And as if in defiance to those around him, Cameron narrowed his gaze on those closest to him. "To Lachlan and Elizabeth!"

"Lachlan and Elizabeth," the crowd responded as they tilted their glasses back, draining the golden liquid in a single swallow.

All eyes turned to Elizabeth, as though challenging her to do the same. She took a deep breath, then tossed back the golden liquor. Instantly a ball of fire spread down her throat and into her chest, sucking the air from her lungs. In spite of the flames that ravaged her insides, Elizabeth held herself upright as she tried not to react. She could hardly breathe, and her knees threatened to buckle, but still she held herself rigid. No one here would see her as weak.

Tears came to her eyes, threatening to spill onto her cheeks. She managed to keep them from betraying her through sheer force of will. She continued to take short, shallow breaths until the embers inside her died down. Who had given her such a strong drink? Usually at these occasions, women were given nothing stronger than hippocras, a drink made from wine, sugar, and spices.

When she could focus on something else besides her own response, Elizabeth looked at the group gathered around. Her gaze caught on Mariam. A satisfied smile tugged at the woman's lips. Elizabeth held that gaze with a challenge in her own. "Thank you for the welcome. Lachlan and I apologize if we kept you waiting for your supper. We've only been married for a few days and have had very little time to ourselves due to travel."

Her eyes narrowing, Mariam stepped forward. "Aye, the newlyweds. You say you've been traveling since you declared yourselves to each other? Perhaps tonight you can have a proper wedding night."

Cheers rose up around them, sending a shiver down Elizabeth's spine. She held herself in check, trying not to let anyone see her response. Lachlan reached for her hand. He held her tight.

"I can take care of my bride, Mariam. Never you mind about that," Lachlan replied.

"If I were your wife," Mariam pressed on, "I would—"

"Fortunately for Lachlan, you are not," Cameron interjected. "Do me a favor, Mariam, and tell Mistress MacInnes we are ready for supper to be served."

Mariam threw Cameron a cold glance before she moved away, her chopines clacking sharply on the floor as she left.

When the others drifted away to take their seats for the

meal, Lachlan held Elizabeth back. "Do not pay any heed to Mariam."

"Were the two of you something more than friends at one point?" Elizabeth boldly asked. She recognized the green eyes of jealousy when she saw them. "That would explain a lot."

He looked surprised. "Nay. Never." When he recovered, he added, "You handled Mariam's taunts and the whisky very well."

Elizabeth shrugged. "I was teased mercilessly by the boys in my clan while growing up. I'm used to being tormented by others."

"That is unacceptable." There was something akin to sympathy in Lachlan's voice. He looked as though he wanted to say more, but Elizabeth quickly changed the subject.

"Why is Mariam here at Ravenscraig Castle? Is she betrothed to Cameron?"

"Nay," Lachlan said. "He was appointed as her guardian when her father was summoned to Edinburgh to become the king's official witch pricker."

"A pricker?" she asked, confused by the odd term.

"He helps identify witches using a special technique called pricking."

Elizabeth shivered. "The witch-hunting that is raging through this country frightens me."

"It should frighten all of us."

Elizabeth clenched her fists, wanting desperately to turn

the conversation to other things. "Shall we take our seats as well? We've kept them from their meal long enough."

Lachlan nodded and guided her toward the seats reserved for them at the head table beside Cameron and his men. Mariam sat at the opposite end of the long table, but that did not stop her from glancing their way time and again while the meal was served.

The meal was an affair of roast stag, three roasted swans, turnips and boiled carrots, onions, leeks, and an assortment of tarts and fresh apples to finish the meal. When they were satiated, the tables were removed and the evening's entertainment began, first with a piper, then with two musicians carrying a flute and a lute, followed by madrigal singers. When the applause and cheers died down, Mariam turned toward Elizabeth and said, "Perhaps Elizabeth could grace us with a song?"

Elizabeth startled and felt a blush come to her cheeks as all eyes once again turned to her. "Nay. I do not like to sing for others."

Mariam narrowed her gaze. "Then you do sing."

"Everyone sings, just not around others," she replied as heat rushed, hotter and brighter, to her cheeks.

"Since you do sing, you should sing for us. After all, this celebration is in your honor. Shouldn't you give something back to those who are celebrating you?" Mariam asked, looking as innocent as a cat with feathers protruding from its mouth.

A round of passionate "ayes" rose around her and Elizabeth felt herself shrinking into a deeper sense of mortification.

"My bride does not need to perform for you," Lachlan said in a stilted voice.

"You're embarrassed for her. How sweet," Mariam said with a self-satisfied smile.

Despite the shivers of apprehension that traveled through Elizabeth, she stood, then moved to the front of the chamber. She drew a deep breath, closed her eyes, and began to sing a Gaelic song her mother had taught her before she'd died. "*A ghaoil, leig dhachaigh gum mhàthair mi.*" She started softly at first, until she opened her eyes to find the others now looked at her not with loathing, but surprise. Feeling more confident, she continued the hypnotic and mysterious song that told of a young girl's encounter with the '*each-uisge*' or water-horse.

When she was done, silence settled all around her until Cameron stood, looking around and clapping. Soon the entire room stood and applauded, all except Mariam, whose features were thunderous.

Cameron came forward and clasped her hands in his. "That song. Where did you learn it?"

"From my mother who learned it from her mother. For generations the women in my family have passed down that song."

Cameron nodded. His eyes were bright and twinkling.

"It awakens the heart to the ages gone by. Well done, Elizabeth."

"Thank you," she stammered, glancing over at Lachlan, more eager than she dared to admit to see his response. But it was a little frightening too, seeing him look at her with confidence in his eyes.

The chairs were removed in preparation for dancing as the piper started to play once more, filling the silence and diverting the attention from her. For that Elizabeth was grateful as she returned to Lachlan's side.

"You're a fine singer. The best I've ever heard."

The words, true or not, ran over her like honey. "Liar," she teased. "But thank you."

Lachlan chuckled and the sound washed over her in another wave of delight. How long had it been since she'd felt such simple pleasure? Too long. The last time she'd sung in a crowd it had been with her mother when she was a child. She had been happy then and had thought the world would always be like that.

It wasn't. When her mother died, she'd learned the hard, cruel reality of life. Her father had tried to comfort her in his own way, but things were never the same.

Regardless of how he meant things, only two days in Lachlan's presence and she'd regained some of the things that had been missing from her life—laughter, belonging, and song. He'd helped guide her back to those things all while she had been nothing but terrible to him. She closed her eyes as a chill replaced her warmth. Then suddenly, she felt a touch against her cheek. She flicked her eyes open.

"Elizabeth?"

"I'm sorry," she interrupted, needing to get her apology off her chest. "I've been horrible to you since the beginning of this journey. That's not me. That's not who I am." She looked around the room at the others who were engaged in conversations and laughing, enjoying themselves. "I was acting as everything they believe a Ruthven to be. But I am not those things. I'm not." She turned back to him, trying to steady the trembling in her fingers, and the quick, loud pounding of her heart.

"We just need to prove that to everyone else." His eyes were sharp reflections of color in the candlelight. And yet, there was a spark of something she hadn't seen in them before—something that pulled at her heart and made her feel warm and shaky again.

He took a half-step toward her. "Elizabeth—"

"Elizabeth." Cameron was suddenly beside them, his face lit with curiosity as his gaze passed between herself and Lachlan. "The dancing is about to start. I would like the first dance to be with you, my lady."

Lachlan stepped back. His eyes shielded now. "Of course. You are the laird of the castle."

Elizabeth felt a stab of regret. Before she could object, Cameron guided her to the middle of the chamber where other dancers had assembled in a line. The musicians were positioned at the back of the chamber, giving the dancers plenty of room to maneuver. The music started and the dance began first with a promenade, then with a twirl of joined hands before they returned to their positions.

She looked for Lachlan. He wasn't dancing. Instead he leaned against the wall, arms crossed over his chest. Blue eyes watched her spin, then dip.

His attention from afar heated her. Suddenly her palms felt moist, her body hot, and her throat breathlessly tight. She forced her gaze away from Lachlan to focus on the motion of her feet. Cameron was an exquisite dancer. He twirled her about and the room flashed by her until she felt not just light-headed, but overly warm. Finally, the music slowed and came to a stop.

She looked over her shoulder trying to locate Lachlan, but he was no longer against the wall. "Thank you for the dance," she said.

"Are you well?" Cameron asked, his brows coming together in a frown. "Your cheeks are flushed red."

"The dancing." She brought her hands up to cover her cheeks. "I must be more tired than I thought."

"Of course." Cameron took her arm and guided her to a chair. He sat her down. "Stay here. I will get you something to drink and find Lachlan."

"Aye," she said as she sank back against the chair, watching her host disappear into the crowd.

In the next moment, Lachlan was beside her. "Elizabeth,

what is wrong?"

She pushed a loose tendril of hair away from her face. Her hands shook slightly. "I'm fine. Simply tired."

Lachlan sat beside her, putting his hand to her forehead. "You feel warm."

"I just need some fresh air and then sleep. It's been a long day."

"Aye, it has." Lachlan stood and offered her his hand. "Come, let's get you some fresh air."

She put her hand in his and let him pull her to her feet. Together they left the great hall, walking slowly, silently, until they stepped into the chill night air in the courtyard. Elizabeth took a deep breath, and let the heather-scented air revive her. She could still hear the skirl of the pipes. She closed her eyes, trying to clear her head and contain the emotions that had tried to break free tonight. She could feel her contempt fading for this man who was her husband. But every time she let someone get close to her, they betrayed her. Every time she gave up a piece of her heart, she got hurt.

Elizabeth fought back the tears that threatened. She turned her head away so that Lachlan could not see them slip onto her cheeks as she remembered snippets from her past.

Most of her father's betrayals had stemmed from the fact she had not been born male. At times, she would think she was finally making headway when he started treating her as his equal, asking for her help in making decisions for the clan. Then, in the next moment, he would call her a know-nothing female, and instead defer to the opinions of other male clan members.

And then there was Roland. He'd fostered with the Ruthvens and been raised as a member of the clan. She and Roland had been inseparable over the past five years and truly devoted to each other, or so she had thought until she learned two of the maids had borne his bastards. Still, she had swallowed her pride and forgave him his indiscretions, hoping someday soon he might ask her father for her hand in marriage. The night she thought he would do just that, he instead told her father he was leaving and had no idea when or if he might return.

The two most important men in her life had betrayed and dismissed her, leaving her feeling alone and unloved.

Forcibly shedding the memories, Elizabeth drew a deep breath, turned her head, and opened her eyes. Lachlan was there in the moonlight, studying her. "If it would help, we can stay here an extra day and let you rest."

The cool breeze fluttered his hair back from his face. It wasn't rest she needed. "Nay, let us continue as you had planned."

He frowned. "If that is what you want."

"It is," she said, the words sounding thin and unconvincing.

Lachlan's frown deepened. "What is it, Elizabeth? What aren't you telling me?"

She turned back to the castle, before he could ask any

further questions, before he could see how vulnerable she felt. For a brief moment tonight, he'd made her feel special, like she was no different than anyone else. But she was. She was a Ruthven. He was a Douglas. She didn't quite know what all that meant anymore, because something inside her had definitely shifted tonight. She and Lachlan were not friends, exactly. Definitely not lovers. But also, not enemies. Could they continue like this, being friendly toward each other while still harboring feelings of resentment and rivalry that had been present their whole lives?

For the short-term, aye. But soon Elizabeth would have to pick a side. Would she remain true to her clan and their desire to keep the Ruthven-Douglas feud going, or would she be the peacemaker the king and queen wanted her to become?

CHAPTER FIVE

UPSTAIRS IN THEIR bedchamber, Lachlan watched Elizabeth from the opposite side of the room. He'd wanted to kiss her after she'd finished her song in the great hall. Her voice had made him feel strangely weak, and filled with an emotion he couldn't quite name. While the applause had sounded around them, he'd seen the look of shocked surprise in her tawny eyes. Innocent and unexpected pleasure. He could spend the rest of his life listening to her sing, watching that joy enter her eyes.

Aye, he'd wanted to kiss her, and so much more. He winced at the memory of the kiss he had forced on her earlier. He should not have done that, but she'd angered him so. He closed his eyes, swallowing back his desire, wishing his own emotions weren't so close to the surface. He groaned. He'd never felt this odd sensation of not quite being in control of his emotions, his reactions.

As a warrior, he usually had a tight rein on his responses. He proceeded with logic and strategy. Around Elizabeth, all of that seemed to flee from his mind as he simply reacted as he never imagined he would.

Lachlan took a deep breath, trying to concentrate on something in the room besides Elizabeth. He stared into the fire, watching the play of light and shadow it cast across the chamber. Until, once again, his gaze returned to her as the light reflected off her hair, making it shimmer with streaks of red and gold as she, too, stared at the flames.

"Since we shall continue our journey in the morning, we should go to sleep," Lachlan said.

Elizabeth lifted her gaze from the fire to look at him in surprise. "There is still so much to—" She stopped, as though suddenly becoming aware of the intimacy of their situation.

Lachlan's gaze clung to the soft rise and fall of her chest as she breathed, the tension in her body as she clutched her hands at her sides, the slight hollow beneath the bones of her cheeks as her lips tightened. And her eyes—as warm as honey on a summer day.

Lachlan jerked his gaze away. "Tomorrow will be another long day of travel."

With a nod she asked, "How shall we sleep tonight?" Her gaze slid toward the overly large bed.

"The bed looks big enough for us both, wouldn't you say? I'll turn my back while you prepare yourself for sleep." He turned to face the wall. There was no sound for a long moment, then finally he heard the rustling of fabric and smelled the warm, sweet scent that belonged to Elizabeth. He closed his eyes, breathing in the aroma, taking it into himself. As he did, a ripple of desire pulsed through him. Her scent wasn't the only part of her he longed to explore. He wanted to join with her, to look at her without all her many layers of clothes. He wanted to touch her—to feel the softness of her skin beneath his calloused palms.

He opened his eyes as he suddenly heard nothing but silence. "Are you finished?"

"I am, my laird." He turned to see her in the bed with the bed sheet pulled up to her chin.

"Lachlan. Only Lachlan. There will never be such formality between us," he said as he took off his belt and sword, then his boots. He set them atop a chair and removed the brooch at his shoulder, releasing the tail of his kilt. He shrugged off his coat and divested himself of his neck scarf before unbuttoning and removing his shirt.

Elizabeth's cheeks flamed red, but she did not look away. Instead her gaze caught on the hair on his chest as it converged in the middle and continued downward. He reached for the thick belt at his waist and slowly unbuckled it. In an instant, his kilt fell to his feet, leaving him naked before her. Her gaze went over him slowly. She could have no doubt that he wanted her, as evidenced by his arousal. She inhaled sharply and finally looked away as she nervously worked her lip between her teeth.

He slipped into the bed beside her. "Goodness, but you are wrapped in the sheet. Loose your hands and let me cover myself."

Instead of releasing the sheet, she pulled it tighter, until he finally pried her hands off the covers and he rolled beneath. For an instant his body touched hers until he pulled away, settling into the rope bed. "There. We are both bedded for the night." He was acutely aware of her, so much so that every nerve in his body was on fire at her nearness. Her sharp intake of breath when he'd accidentally touched her sent his pulse racing. He struggled to master his desire, willing himself to think of other things . . . like the dangers ahead of them on their journey tomorrow. "You've nothing to fear from me, Elizabeth. Turn over and try to sleep."

Elizabeth lay as still as stone beside him. "Does that mean that you won't . . . that we won't . . ."

"I made you a promise."

She turned to him. The relief on her face faded as she suddenly paled. "The others are expecting us to have a true wedding night." She sat up and for a moment the sheet dropped, exposing the sheer white chemise through which he could see the small tipped peaks of her breasts. "If there is no evidence of our joining, Mariam will be the first to cry out that I am proved unchaste."

He sat up and tried to make out her features in the dying embers of the fire. She appeared quite pale in the flickering light. "No one is to say you are unchaste other than myself. Only I have the right to say how you came to me. Let us be done with this subject. Now lie down and get some rest."

Still she hesitated. "Have you had much experience with

women?"

He startled. What was she asking if he was a virgin?

He must have let his surprise register on his face because her eyes went wide as she clarified, "I mean, do you know how women think? Or how devious some of them can be?"

Lachlan relaxed. "I had no sisters and have spent the better part of my life only around men, especially my brothers-in-arms."

"If you intend to leave me chaste, then might I suggest we find some blood?" She offered her palm as she had the night before. "A small amount will do."

With a sigh, he rolled to sit at the side of the bed, then stood. He strode to the chair containing his abandoned clothing. He dressed quickly in his shirt and kilt. Finally, he thrust his feet into his boots and turned to face her once more.

"Where are you going? You said we needed sleep," Elizabeth asked.

"I'll be back."

"If I've offended you, I am sorry."

"You are an odd one, Elizabeth. I will grant you that," he said as he slipped from the room. He managed a smile as he made his way down the back stairs. It wouldn't do for someone to see him. If they did, his nighttime journey would be all for naught.

But he need not have worried because no one was about. They had either taken to their beds or were still in the great hall. He quickly found what he needed and made his way back to the bedchamber. As he shut the door behind him, he heard an odd sound.

Croak. Croak. Croak.

As soon as he stepped away from the door the sound stopped. "What was that?" he asked.

Elizabeth sat against the pillows, watching him with wary eyes as he approached the bed with a pail. "I'm fairly certain it is exactly what it sounds like—frogs."

"Someone put frogs in this room?"

"Aye."

"Whatever for?"

"To remind me once again that I am not wanted here."

"God's teeth," he swore and set the bucket down. "I'll find the frogs and return them to the outside."

"Nay," Elizabeth protested. "I do not mind the sound. In fact, I find it rather comforting."

He frowned. "You do?"

She nodded. "It reminds me of summers near the loch, when I would lie on the shore, looking up at the stars and listening to the soft repetitive croaking of the frogs. If you close your eyes, you can imagine them serenading you."

He gave her a skeptical look, then grinned. "I suppose one can imagine anything if one tries hard enough."

She smiled in return. "At least Mariam didn't place an adder in the sheets."

His grin vanished. "You think Mariam did this?"

"I suspect it," Elizabeth said then gestured to the bucket. "What is that?"

"Get up for a moment," he replied, taking the bucket in his hands once more.

She wrapped the bed sheet around her and rolled to the edge just as he poured the contents of the bucket in the middle of the lower bed linens. She gaped at him in horror as a red splotch of color darkened the cloth. "What did you do?"

"You wanted blood. I got some from the slaughter-house." He gestured toward the bed again. "Now get back in bed."

Her eyes went wide. "I'll not sleep in blood."

He shook his head, dazed by the conversation. "First you want blood. Then you don't want blood. Which is it to be?"

"Whose blood is that?"

"It's the stag's blood from our meal tonight. I gathered some of the blood they set aside." He stared down at the bright red splotch. "Do you think it's enough?"

"Sweet Mary . . . 'tis more than enough. They will definitely think I surrendered my maidenhead, but they will also think you abused me all night."

He frowned. He had no idea how much blood would be spilled by a virgin on her wedding night. All he knew was war. And to him, what was on the bed was hardly any blood at all. "Well, that amount will have to do since there is no taking it back." With a shrug, he hid the bucket inside the armoire in the corner of the chamber. "I'll return this to the slaughterhouse in the morn." Turning back to the bed, he peeled out of his clothing then slid onto the soiled sheet, pulling the coverlet over himself. "You can stand there freezing all night, or you can lie beside me and warm yourself. I intend to get some sleep while I still can." He turned on his side and, propping his head on his elbow, looked up at her. "You did well tonight, Elizabeth. I doubt other women would have done so well given the challenges you faced first with the whisky, then the singing, and now with the frogs."

Hot color stained her cheeks. "Thank you," she said, her voice so quiet he had to strain to hear it. She hesitated another moment before she finally lay back down on the bed and pulled the coverlet over her body, shielding herself from his gaze.

The fire crackled, the light passing over her face, brightening her eyes, her cheekbones, her lips. She was so lovely when she was at peace like this. Peace between a Ruthven and a Douglas. Who would have thought it would only take a few days to accomplish such a feat? Pleasure wound through him, spiraling until it became a smile tugging at the corners of his mouth.

In the half-light he relaxed back into his pillow and listened to the croaking of the frogs. She was right. The sound was soothing. "Tell me about your summers by the loch."

"You wish to hear about that? Something from my past

as a Ruthven?" she asked nervously.

"There is no Ruthven or Douglas in this room tonight. Only two people who are curious about each other. Tell me about the loch."

She relaxed into the softness of the mattress. She laughed nervously. "You truly wish to know about my past?"

"Aye."

There was another short pause before she drew a deep breath and said, "As a child I was drawn to the water of the loch near our home. At sunset the water would turn from green to black, and the frogs that had been hidden from view all day would come to the shoreline . . ."

CHAPTER SIX

LACHLAN HAD ENCOURAGED Elizabeth to talk too long the night before. Even so, they were on their way at sunrise, shortly after Lachlan had secretly returned the bucket to the slaughterhouse. They had bid their farewells before much of the household had awakened, a fact with which Elizabeth was well pleased. It meant avoiding further challenges by the residents of Ravenscraig or any possible comments about the amount of blood in her and Lachlan's bed.

Involuntarily, her thoughts returned to last night. Despite all the challenges the residents of Ravenscraig had thrown at her, she had passed their tests. Her small victory brought a surge of satisfaction she had not experienced before. Lachlan had been proud of her. She was surprised at how happy the thought made her as the next segment of their journey began.

Lachlan had opted to leave the carriage behind for his coachman and Cameron's men to deliver to Whittingehame at a later date, and instead to proceed on horseback for which Elizabeth was grateful since it meant she no longer needed to suggest such a tactic.

There was no sign of her father or his men this morning, but Elizabeth could not help but think they weren't far away. Donald Ruthven was no fool. It wouldn't have taken him long to figure out the deception of yesterday's travel. At least on horseback, she and Lachlan could stay ahead of the Ruthvens if they picked up their pace.

Elizabeth nudged her horse into a slightly faster rhythm.

Lachlan increased his speed to match hers. "Are you in a hurry to put Ravenscraig behind us?"

She turned in her saddle to look at the landscape behind her, searching for her father's presence. Finding none, she released a shattered breath. Just because she could not see her father and his men as she had before did not mean they were not there. "Lachlan, I . . ." She'd been trying to find a way to tell him about her father following them all morning, but had yet to find the words. "I need to tell—"

"Since you are not afraid of the water," Lachlan said, interrupting her, "I've decided we should cross the Firth of Forth instead of taking the longer journey around."

Elizabeth nearly sagged with relief. Again, Lachlan had spared her from formulating a half-truth or from betraying her clan. "I've never been on a boat before."

"It's more of a ship than a boat," he corrected. "Large enough for a full crew, cargo, and several horses."

Elizabeth pulled the edges of her cloak together against the cool morning air. "How long will it take us to cross the

Firth?"

"With the winds to the southeast and in our favor, it should only take a few hours to reach the shores of Aberlady. We save a day and a half of travel taking this route."

Her father would never expect them to sail instead of traveling by land. Pleased at the turn of events, Elizabeth kept her confession to herself. As the morning mist dissipated, the blue-green waters of the Firth of Forth came into view. Traveling closer to Kirkcaldy Beach, Elizabeth soon made out a long, narrow dock and a ship with three tall masts anchored there.

"Is that the ship we will be taking?" she asked as Lachlan brought his horse alongside hers.

Lachlan nodded. "She's a carrack named *The Golden Rose*. Cameron Sinclair owns this ship and several others."

"He's a merchant?" Elizabeth asked.

Lachlan raised a brow. "He's a warrior who dabbles in trade with exotic locales."

"That explains the spices used on the roasted stag last night. I have never tasted their like."

"Cinnamon."

"What?" she asked.

"It's the inner bark of a tree. Cameron has developed quite a fondness for the spice. He's acquired that and many others from a trade route out of Egypt."

"I've heard tales of great explorers who have sailed vast distances and discovered many wondrous treasures."

"Aye," Lachlan said. "Places filled with silver and gold, forests that go on forever, and many native cultures, in addition to many pleasurable things such as cinnamon."

She nodded. "There is so much out there, so many things we have yet to discover or to even imagine."

"You sound like an explorer," he said.

"I have always been interested in what lies beyond the horizon. We live on an island, and there is so much more to see beyond the Scottish shores." She became thoughtful for a moment. "Perhaps that is why I am drawn to water . . ."

"It sounds as though I should talk with Cameron about letting the two of us sail on one of his ships as it travels to foreign lands. Would you like that?"

She would love to travel, but she wasn't certain if she wanted to travel with him. "I will think about it."

Neither said anything further until they reached the coast where Lachlan dismounted then lifted Elizabeth down from her horse. "God's teeth, you're cold. Why didn't you tell me you were so cold?" He pulled her cloak more closely around her.

"I didn't feel the cold after a while," she replied as the wind continued to blow all around her.

He removed his own cloak and settled it over her shoulders before he enfolded her in his arms. "This should help you stay warm until I can get the horses settled on the ship."

She tensed at first, then unable to resist the warmth lingering on Lachlan's cloak as it permeated through to her flesh, she relaxed. She should back away, refuse to take the comfort he offered, but she found she could not. Instead, she focused on the howling of the wind as it whipped across the Firth. Whitecaps danced on the surface, giving evidence of the strength of the wind. "Will it be safe to cross in this weather?"

"It is always a little windy here at the Firth. And 'tis nothing to a large ship like *The Golden Rose*."

"Thank you for the warning," she said after a long moment.

"I will see you safely across."

She looked down at his chest, refusing to meet his eyes. "I used to think I didn't need anyone or anything in my life—that I was fine being alone, being ignored by my clan, being unloved by my father. He wanted a son, you know. He was never pleased that I was his only child."

"You were his child. That should have been enough. He should love you for who you are."

"Love?" She startled at the word. "Do men know the meaning of the word?"

He pulled back to look into her face. "Aye, Elizabeth, they do. I've seen that miracle twice recently with my cousins, Reid and Quinn. I cannot wait for you to meet them and the women who stole their hearts, Lucy and Vivian. You'll like them."

He was talking to her as though she were a part of his family, not a stranger who he did not truly know. Tears sprang to her eyes and ran down her cheeks, only to be whipped away by the wind. "I don't know why I'm crying," she said as she impatiently wiped her wet cheeks. "It's foolish to weep over the past." And maybe even the future. Would Lachlan's family treat her the same way the residents of Ravenscraig Castle had? She couldn't change who she was. Or could she?

He didn't comment on her crying. He merely held her until her tears dried up. When she was at peace once more, he loosened his arms and took her hand, leading her to a log that sat facing the water on the beach. "Sit here and wait until I load the horses, then we will set sail."

As she watched Lachlan head toward the boat, she wondered what it would have been like to be loved by a father. If he had loved her, would it have made a difference in her life from the start? If she had learned to trust love instead of reject it? She was finding it harder and harder to see Lachlan as her father had always painted their enemy—as ruthless and dangerous. Instead, the longer they were together she saw him as caring and almost tender. Was that what a man who could love was like? She'd thought Roland had shown her love before, but perhaps true love was something bigger than she'd ever imagined.

LESS THAN AN hour later, with the wind in her face, Elizabeth curled her hand around the rail on *The Golden Rose*'s forecastle. She gazed at the tall, round masts and the sails that were taut, filled with wind as they made their way across the Firth of Forth. The water below was turbulent, but the ship remained steady, lifting then falling in a constant rhythm. Below her, sailors darted to and fro as they adjusted the sails and tightened the rigging. It was like a well-orchestrated dance between the wind and the men who chose to capture it, however briefly, to do their bidding.

"The wind is sharpening. You should go below deck." Lachlan came to stand beside her.

"Soon," she replied. "I like it here." She gazed out at the point where the sea met the sky and listened to the wind as it sang through the rigging. "I feel like everything is so clear out here on the water. Like nothing is hidden from view except what lies beyond the horizon." She turned to him with a smile. "But that is where the mystery begins. There is so much promise beyond that horizon."

He studied her expression. "You are a sailor at heart."

She turned back to look at the horizon and felt her exhilaration fade. "Except that women have no place on a journey of exploration. Their place is at home, surrounded by chi—"

"Your place," Lachlan interrupted, "is wherever you choose it to be."

She gazed at him incredulously. "You truly believe that?"

"Of course. Life is short and often filled with difficulty. It is our dreams that make our lives worth living."

"Is it your dream to be a warrior and protect the king?"

His lips tightened. "I do what I do out of loyalty to my kin and my country, and because I have never had any reason to do anything else." His voice faded as he looked out at the water, suddenly tense.

"Excuse me, Elizabeth," he said before he rushed to the back of the forecastle and stared into the distance. "There's a boat in distress to our starboard side. They are sinking."

"Fishermen?" one of the seamen asked as he came to join Lachlan at the railing.

"Most likely," Lachlan replied. "And if we do not hurry, they will all drown."

The seaman shouted orders to reduce the sail, which slowed the ship. The swells seemed large now that *The Golden Rose* wasn't gliding over their tops. In the distance, Elizabeth could see an overturned boat with six men struggling to keep their heads above water as they clung to the wood. It seemed to take forever to get *The Golden Rose* into position alongside their small boat.

"Bring her up close," the captain commanded the seaman at the rudder.

"Aye, Captain," he shouted and put the ship into a quick turn that sent white water along the lee rail. As they got closer to the men in distress, several seamen who could swim leapt into the water, Lachlan among them.

By the time they arrived at the scene, only four men remained above the water, clinging to the boat. Elizabeth's breath stilled in her chest as she watched Lachlan dive below the water's surface, no doubt looking for the two men who had vanished beneath the waves. Long horrible moments passed while the sodden men were lifted out of the water and hauled onto the quarterdeck by those who had remained aboard.

Where was Lachlan? She could see nothing in the water, which now appeared an inky black. Finally, a dark-colored head broke through the choppy surface, followed by a more familiar one. Relief ran through Elizabeth's blood so potently she felt dizzy. Lachlan was all right and he had saved one of the men who would have drowned.

The seamen at the rail lowered a boat hook that Lachlan attached to the fisherman's clothing. They hauled him up. His body was limp, his face white, and he was streaming with water when they deposited him on the deck. The seamen pumped the man's legs up toward his head, hoping to rid him of the seawater he had breathed. After several attempts, the man coughed, sputtered and gave up the water in his lungs. Color returned to his face as he struggled to open his eyes.

In the meanwhile, Lachlan dove beneath the surface once more, continuing his search. He came to the surface and dove down again. He did so four more times before the captain shouted for the men to haul Lachlan back on board. Of the six, five had been saved.

There was a strained quietness when Lachlan returned on

deck. His clothes were plastered to his well-muscled chest and thighs, and he too was streaming with water before a seaman dropped a blanket about his shoulders.

"You gave it a good try, m'laird." Another seaman clapped Lachlan on the shoulder.

"'Twas obviously the man's time to meet his maker," yet another said.

Lachlan nodded solemnly then turned to the five men huddled on the deck, wrapped in blankets. "What was his name?" he asked, his voice oddly hoarse.

"Dillon Kemp," one of the men replied, turning to face Lachlan.

A muscle jerked in Lachlan's jaw. "I shall remember him with a prayer."

LACHLAN LOOKED BACK toward Elizabeth. He saw the distressed look on her face and felt every muscle in his body tense as he fought the urge to go to her and in front of all these men, pull her into his arms. But he would not drown her in embarrassment. There had been one too many drownings today already.

Even so, her gaze clung to his—as though asking for something, but what, he had no idea. Finally, she glanced away and stepped back as the captain approached.

"Let us get these men below deck and into dry clothing,"

the captain barked at the seamen closest to the fishermen. "Everyone else, resume your stations. There is nothing else for us to do here. Fill the sails and let's be on our way."

As the fishermen stood and moved to follow the seamen below deck, one man paused as his gaze lit on Elizabeth. "Lizzie! Sweet Lizzie, is that you?" The dark-haired young man moved toward Elizabeth.

Lachlan saw Elizabeth's eyes widen in recognition. "Roland Carswell?"

"Aye, Lizzie! God's teeth, but you are a welcome sight!" the young man cried out as he enveloped her in a wet embrace.

Elizabeth's eyes sparkled with unshed tears. "How was it you were on that boat, Roland? I am so relieved you are safe."

Lachlan stared at Elizabeth, locked in the young man's embrace, and felt suddenly heavy inside. Obviously the two were friends. And from the looks of it possibly even more than that.

"After years of searching for my purpose, I've decided to become a minister. The king approves. He is sending me to the University of Edinburgh to train. I sought passage across the Firth with these men in order to save more of the stipend I was given."

With a soft smile, Elizabeth put her hand against Roland's cheek. "I'm pleased you found a purpose in this life, but trying to be thrifty almost cost you your life."

Roland placed his hand over hers, and Elizabeth's cheeks grew pink and her breath hitched. Lachlan took a step toward her then forced himself to pause, despite the strange urge inside to rush forward and grab her away.

"What were you doing so far from home?" Roland asked. "You never leave the safety of your clan."

Elizabeth cast a furtive glance Lachlan's way. "I'm married now."

Lachlan felt a momentary respite. At least she had admitted to someone from her past her new status.

"Married?" Roland's eyes filled with challenge as his hand dropped from her face. He turned toward Lachlan. "You would force your beautiful wife on such a dangerous journey?"

"I'm not forcing her to do anything. And, if you must know, we are headed to our new home . . . together."

"Is this true, Elizabeth? Do you want to go with this man?" Roland asked, his voice filled with scorn. "There was a time when your dreams were all for me."

"You left Perthshire, Roland. You left me behind."

His features hardened. "I had to if I was ever going to become my own man. I had hoped you would wait for me."

Elizabeth looked away. "Things change." Her tone was brusque. "Besides, you have your new life as a minister to look forward to. That's what you always wanted . . . to guide the spiritual lives of those for whom you care."

Roland threw Lachlan a cold look before he captured

Elizabeth's chin with his fingers, returning her gaze to his. "I'd always pictured you as part of that life."

Elizabeth stepped back, forcing Roland to release her. She moved to Lachlan's side, standing close but not quite touching him. "Lachlan Douglas is my new life."

Roland's eyes seemed to bulge in his face. "You married a Douglas? Your father agreed to this union?"

"Aye. As did the king and queen. I had no choice but to do as they bid me. No matter how much I might wish otherwise, this is a man's world and women have few choices about their own lives."

Lachlan clenched his teeth, ignoring the disquieting feeling settling in his gut. He wanted to argue that Elizabeth had far more choices with him than she had ever had within the confines of her clan. But that was not something he could make her accept. She had to come to the conclusion herself, no matter how long it took.

"The crossing is getting rough," Lachlan said, ignoring the wild mixture of emotions tearing through him that he was half-afraid to examine. It did not matter that Roland and Elizabeth had a past. He and Elizabeth had a past as well, but he doubted she remembered as much. Besides, Elizabeth was his wife. For better or worse. "You should join the others below deck." Lachlan had barely finished speaking when the ship pitched suddenly. Before Elizabeth lost her balance, he pulled her against his chest and wrapped his arms around her, holding her steady as the iron and wooden ship shuddered.

The ship rocked again and Roland was thrown sideways. He clutched the rail, avoiding a second spill into the dark waters.

"With the winds to the southeast, the waves will only get stronger and the wind more forceful as we approach Aberlady's coastline," Lachlan said, still holding Elizabeth tight against his chest. "The captain does not need any distractions if he is to keep us from being blown against the rocks or caught on a sandbar outside the bay."

Roland gained his balance. He glared at Lachlan one more time before he staggered toward the hatch leading to safety below deck.

When he was gone, Lachlan loosened his hold on Elizabeth. She did not pull away. Instead, she studied him defiantly as she ran nervous fingers through her tousled brown hair, trying to tame it in the wind. "You needn't glare at me. I did not know we would cross paths with Roland."

"His presence changes nothing. We will leave him in Aberlady and continue as we had planned."

"But—"

"There is nothing to discuss here, Elizabeth." His tone was soft but edged with steel. "You and I have our plans. Roland has his own."

She started to speak but he stopped her.

"Leave things as they are."

Pink rose to color her cheeks. Her gaze clung to his and

suddenly he was startled to see her bravado fade into wariness. She looked hurriedly away and gave an uncaring shrug. "As you wish."

Lachlan stared at the stubborn, willful, and exasperating woman before him. None of this was *as he wished*. If things were as he wished the two of them would be safely back at Whittingehame and a willing Elizabeth would be in his bed, ready to begin their new lives together.

CHAPTER SEVEN

*T*HE *GOLDEN ROSE* dropped anchor outside the Bay of Aberlady. Those aboard who were not continuing on to Spain were tendered the short distance to shore. Elizabeth sat in the boat along with the fishermen and Roland, while Lachlan swam with the horses to the sandy beach.

Instead of watching the man swimming beside the boat, Elizabeth looked to the sand and the dunes beyond. The golden sand seemed to go on forever, only relieved by green grass and windblown shrubs farther away from shore. In the distance, she could see several buildings. It was common for there to be not only an inn, but also a stable in these seaside towns for travelers by sea or over land to utilize. No doubt, they would make use of them both.

When they reached the beach, one of the seamen stepped out of the boat, then offered Elizabeth a hand so she could do the same. Or at least the seaman tried to help her until Roland edged the young man out of the way. "Allow me," Roland said, assisting her as she stepped onto the golden sand.

The fishermen scrambled over the side of the boat themselves, grateful to once again be on land.

Finally, Lachlan and the horses emerged from the water.

The afternoon sun shone brightly overhead, taking the edge off the wind when Lachlan and the horses emerged from the water. Sunbeams glinted off beads of water that rolled down his bare torso. The sea had molded his breeches to his long, powerful legs. For a moment his eyes met hers before he turned to the horses. "Well done," he said in a soothing tone to the animals.

Jolted by the sight of him naked from the waist up this time in the bright light of day, she swallowed roughly. His back was to her and she could see his muscles rippling as he stroked first one wet neck and then the other. Both horses responded by rubbing their muzzles against his broad shoulders.

He chuckled then raked his hands through his hair to remove a bright shower of excess droplets, before heading to the boat where he plucked his shirt off one of the wooden benches. After he slipped the garment over his head, his gaze met hers once more. Hot color rose to her cheeks and spread down her throat.

He said nothing as he returned to the horses, grabbing their reins in either hand before coming to stop before her. He handed her one set of reins. "We'll need to give the horses a rest, and allow them time to eat before we continue." He pointed to a wooden structure in the near distance. "There's a stable up there where the horses can get feed and water. And we should be able to find something to eat at The Cairn Inn next door."

Before she could comment, he moved away toward where the fishermen stood talking among themselves about how they would return to their homes. "Follow us to the inn and I will pay for you to stay there tonight then leave at dawn with another fishing vessel."

Thomas, the fisherman who almost drowned, stepped forward with a frown. "Our families will be worried if we dinna return tae them by nightfall. And Dillon's mother deserves tae ken she lost her son tae the waters of the Firth."

Lachlan placed a hand on the young man's shoulder. "If you return by water tonight, in this wind, you all might join Dillon in his watery grave."

Continuing to frown, Thomas returned to the others. The four men gathered close, discussing their options. After a time, Thomas turned back around. "Yer right. We should-na push our luck too far fer one day."

Lachlan nodded. "Your families will be overjoyed to see you on the morrow."

"Aye," they all agreed.

Lachlan signaled them to head up the bluff, toward the building in the distance. He waited for Elizabeth to lead her horse up the path first, when Roland strode up beside her.

Her heart sank but she offered him a tight smile. As much as she had thought she loved Roland in the past, his presence irritated her now. She'd never realized how much he expected from her—her attention, her laughter, her agreement with everything he said or did. But at least she knew how to deal with him. He was safe, predictable, familiar, and . . . so unlike her husband.

She looked back over her shoulder at the man behind her and a fresh stab of confusion moved through her. She still didn't trust him, but she'd seen a different side of him on their journey across the Firth. He'd been brave beyond compare to dive into the icy water and save the fishermen. He'd been relentless in his efforts to try to bring Dillon back from a watery grave. He'd been protective of her when the ship had encountered extreme weather, and yet she'd also seen a strange vulnerability in his eyes every time Roland drew near.

Elizabeth pushed thoughts of her husband aside, refusing to allow him to disturb her. Forcing interest into her voice she turned to Roland. "Will you stay in Aberlady for the night along with the fishermen, or continue on to Edinburgh?"

"Since I cannot make it all the way to the city before nightfall, I think it would be best to stay and start off fresh in the morning," Roland replied as they continued up the path with the horse trailing behind them. He leaned closer to her, touching her arm. "Why are you with that . . . traitor? Leave him. Come with me."

"Nay, Roland." Elizabeth gently pulled her arm away.

"Why are you loyal to a man who is supposed to be your

enemy?" She saw pleading in his brown eyes. "I can offer you so much more, give you the life you deserve."

"I'm married, Roland. Not even you can change that fact." Elizabeth looked back over her shoulder once more and met Lachlan's disconcerting gaze. An uncomfortable wave of guilt came over her at the realization she had considered Roland's offer for a heartbeat before dismissing it. Her response surprised and confused her. Quickly, she glanced away, summoning indifference. "Your path takes you to Edinburgh, Roland, mine to Whittingehame Castle. I don't want to discuss this anymore."

Roland's eyes were dark. "Very well then, I will continue on to Edinburgh and my studies there. But if you should ever need my assistance, only send word and I will come for you wherever you are."

She nodded then looked down at her feet as they crested the sandy trail and came up onto the solid, grassy turf. At the smell of grass, the mare's slow plodding changed to a quick walk, taking Elizabeth with her as she moved toward the tufts of green grass. Giving the hungry horse a moment to graze, with relieved regret she watched Roland stride away toward the inn.

Lachlan came up beside her. "Come, let us give the horses a rest while we dine. We have a hard and fast trip ahead of us if we are to make our destination by nightfall." He turned to the fishermen. "Wait here. My wife and I must settle the horses, then we'll go together to the inn. Your meal and your stay will be at my expense."

The fishermen thanked him. A moment later Lachlan and his mare set off in the direction of a well-maintained stable. He was several paces ahead of her when Elizabeth followed. There was an edge to his words, despite his civility. She frowned. Her conversation with Roland had obviously upset him. But why? She was still here with him. That should have pleased him at least a little bit. Grumbling to herself, she entered the stable after him and led her horse to Lachlan.

He took the reins from her and proceeded to remove the bridle and saddle from her horse before guiding it to a feeder he filled with several scoops of oats. The horses ate hungrily. "Why don't you wait outside with the fishermen. I'll meet you there in a moment after I replenish the water in the trough."

"I could help."

"I can accomplish the task faster on my own."

She stiffened, feeling strangely abandoned. "I apologize for inconveniencing you."

He frowned. "Why are you angry with me?"

Her lashes fell to veil the anger and uncertainty in her eyes. "I would not dare be angry with you."

"You'd dare." He looked at her an instant before returning to his work. "I apologize if I seem terse. This morning has not exactly turned out as we'd planned."

"Nay, it has not."

His gaze connected with hers once more. "What do you say we call a truce?"

She nodded. "Truce."

A rare smile lit his face. "Good. I'll be outside in no time at all," he said, picking up a bucket and heading toward the nearby well.

She turned and headed back toward the stable door. He was a difficult man to understand, she thought wearily. At times he was all sharp edges, driven by duty and honor. At other times he was gentle and almost kind. And his smile . . . it had been beautiful and directed at her alone.

Elizabeth swallowed, pushing the thought away before it could stretch into something more. She took a quick step, then stopped dead in her tracks as a thin black cat, with a long, wiry tail leapt into her path. Its green eyes stared up at her as though appraising her. "Shoo," she said, flicking her hand away from herself with the hope it would clear her path.

The black cat moved, but not in the direction she had intended. Instead it brushed up against her legs and began to purr. She wanted to be irritated with the beast, but found she could not. Instead, she bent down and gently stroked its back. Instantly the animal arched higher, as though begging for more of the same. "Are you starved for affection?" she asked, continuing to stroke the cat from its head to its tail. "Or are you simply starved? No mice in the stable to catch?"

Loud purring issued from the beast.

Elizabeth couldn't help but smile as she stood once more. "Come with me. I'll see if the innkeeper has a few scraps to spare for you."

The cat gratefully followed beside her out of the stable. As she moved to join the others, her smile faded as the fishermen's gazes passed between herself and the black cat. Their faces blanched. "*Go bhfóire dia orainn!*" Thomas exclaimed, calling upon God to help them as he turned and chattered excitedly to the others.

As the cat continued to rub against her legs, Elizabeth clenched her fingers. A shiver went up her spine. "What's wrong, Thomas?"

He turned to her, his eyes dark and unfathomable. "We're leaving, regardless of the dangers. None of us will be beholden tae one such as yer husband." His voice quivered with fear. He and the men did not walk, they ran back to the beach.

"Thomas, wait—" Before she could finish her words, they disappeared down the path. Unaffected by the men's odd behavior, the cat continued to purr and stroked its own back against the skirt of her gown. "What got into them?" she asked the beast, bending down to rub its neck. The men were scared, but of what? A cat? Her? The fear that their families might assume they were all dead? She was still pondering the situation, when Lachlan joined her outside.

"Where are Thomas and the others?" Lachlan asked with a frown.

She stood. "Something frightened them when I came out of the stable with this cat. They decided to make their own way back across the channel now instead of waiting for the wind to settle."

"Black cats are an omen of doom for fishermen. Many will not travel by boat for an entire day when a black cat crosses their path." He shrugged though his features were tight as he gazed at the choppy water in the distance. "We cannot stop them if they choose to return home tonight. They know the dangers, not from the presence of a black cat, but from the weather." After a long moment he said, "Come, let us eat so we can be on our way ourselves." He looked down, then bent and scratched the affectionate cat behind the ears. "Looks like you have a friend."

"I cannot believe the men would be so frightened of a cat."

"'Tis superstitious nonsense." Lachlan stood. "Since King James set up his witch tribunals there are many men and women who suddenly believe a black cat is either a servant of a witch or a witch themselves in familiar form."

"'Tis only a barn cat," Elizabeth replied.

"To you and me, aye. But again, we cannot control what others believe." Lachlan started toward the inn. Elizabeth and the black cat both followed. With the cat at her side, Elizabeth felt her steps lighten. If she were honest, she was eager—almost excited—to get on with the final leg of their journey. Was she more relaxed now because her father and his men were no longer on their heels? Or because Roland, the man she had once hoped to be her future, had left her and all of his empty promises behind? He had betrayed her before. She would not give him an opportunity to do so again.

Elizabeth lifted her skirts and ran to catch up with Lachlan. Now that she had parted ways both mentally and physically with Roland, she could move on with her future. Perhaps she could think of this moment as a fresh start. At the door of the small inn, Lachlan stepped back, allowing her to enter before him. The interior was clean and a cheerful fire burned in the stone fireplace in the common room. The delicious aroma of roasting hare drifted to Elizabeth from a spit over the fire that was turned by a serving maid.

The innkeeper hurried forward, a toothless grin lighting his round face. "Welcome, m'laird, milady." He bowed then asked, "How might I be of service today?"

"I left two horses in your stable with feed and water, and my good wife and I desire a plate of the roasted hare, if you please. I'll pay extra for a scrap or two to be placed outside for the cat."

"Of course," he said, nodding. "Come, sit here and we will serve you at once, m'laird." The innkeeper showed them to a table near the fire, then snapped his fingers, gaining the maid's attention. The young woman left the spit and hurried toward them with two mugs of wine she set before them, then returned with two plates of meat, mashed turnips, and a slice of rustic bread slathered in butter.

Elizabeth had not realized how hungry she had become until the food was before her. Her mouth watered at the sight of meat, roasted to perfection. With her fork in her left hand and knife in her right, she cut off a small bite and placed it on her tongue. With an effort, she held back a groan of pleasure. Elizabeth could feel Lachlan's gaze on her face but avoided looking up to meet his eyes. The common room buzzed with the hum of conversation between others who had stopped for a meal, yet silence stretched between herself and Lachlan.

Why did he not speak? It was obvious he had questions about Roland. When the silence stretched on, she realized she would have to be the one to break it. "You have nothing to worry about with regards to Roland. He is an old friend, but anything between us is over."

"Are you so certain of that? Roland appears to have differing thoughts on that matter."

A frown furrowed her brow. "It matters not what he thinks. I am your wife. We can hardly change that fact."

He smiled cynically. "For some men, even that is no obstacle." His wooden chair creaked as he leaned back and stretched his long legs out before him, his gaze on the fire.

"Roland goes to Edinburgh to study to be a minister."

Lachlan's lips tightened. "That makes him even more dangerous given the current political climate. Ministers are encouraged by King James to rid their kirks of those who are seen as disturbers of the status quo."

"I don't understand what that has to do with anything."

"Don't you?" he asked with a bitter tone in his voice. "Anyone whom the ministers want to be rid of may be charged as a witch or a warlock, and few who are charged escape a painful death."

Elizabeth did not have to ask the nature of their deaths. She'd heard about the ruthless burnings of both men and women all over Scotland since the Berwick witch trials began. The old, infirm, and those touched by madness had been preyed upon the most because of their inability to resist the horrific torture they'd had to endure. "Roland would never accuse an innocent person," she argued.

"From what I saw of him in the last few hours, that young man looked like he would do anything to get you away from a Douglas."

At his words, she drank the last of her wine before setting the wooden goblet down on the table. "I still do not believe Roland could be so cruel, but just to be certain we had best be on our way and get you to Whittingehame Castle's protection before nightfall."

He smiled crookedly. "Wife, you sound as if you care."

She pushed back her chair and stood. She did care, but she would never tell him that. "I already have a husband. I would be very put out if I had to find myself another."

He stood and took a step toward her and she caught the scent of the sea and the summer sunshine that clung to his skin. He brought his fingers up to caress her cheek and jawline. "I'm going to pretend it is because you care for me more than you are willing to say." His smile was purely sensual.

She inhaled sharply and a shiver ran through her.

For a heartbeat, he gazed into her eyes as though looking for proof of what she denied before he dropped his hand to his side. "Do you need to refresh yourself or shall we be on our way?"

"I am ready to go."

"Very well. We won't stop until we reach Whittinge-hame."

CHAPTER EIGHT

THE PURPLE LIGHT of dusk veiled the world around them and Elizabeth worried that they would not make it to the castle before nightfall. The journey to Whittinge-hame had been as grueling as Lachlan had predicted. He'd ridden beside her, but he'd uttered not a word. Was he lost in thoughts of what lay ahead for them once they reached his home? For that was where her thoughts began and ended. What would happen once they reached their destination?

Half an hour later as the sky changed to a purplish gray a square, battlemented keep, three stories high appeared ahead of them. A woodland spread for miles behind the structure and a river flowed past on the west. The land of her new home was not only beautiful, it appeared to be fertile as well.

"'Twas built three hundred years back." Lachlan finally spoke to her as they passed through two barbican towers with gates swung wide open as if in welcome. Behind that came a portcullis with its massive grille of iron spikes. As they continued forward, a guardsman saluted Lachlan. An instant later, the metal gate came down to seal the entryway behind them.

The clip-clop of horse hooves echoed all around them as they crossed over the planked drawbridge and entered the outer bailey. "On a clear day," he continued, raising his voice to counter the sound, "the view extends as far as Arthur's Seat to the northwest. The woodlands are good for gaming, and there is plenty of water flowing through the glen below. The castle is an easily defensible fortress. In case you were worried about such things."

"That is nice to know in case my—"

"In case your father should attack?" he finished her sentence for her.

Elizabeth's eyes went wide. "You knew?"

"I knew he'd been following us since we left Falkland Palace. 'Tis another reason we traveled by sea. Your father and his men could not follow without exposing themselves."

"I did not ask them to follow me," she replied defensively.

"I do not blame him. Or you." He turned his attention back to the path they traveled through the bailey. "I would do the same in his position."

Elizabeth frowned. "What will you do when he does arrive?"

"Talk to him like the warriors we are, and hopefully come to a resolution that doesn't involve either of our deaths." He turned to her again, this time his eyes filled not with anger, but with possession. "You are my wife, Elizabeth, and no one will hurt you again, including your father."

Her breath stilled in her chest. "What if his motives are less than honorable?" She wouldn't put it past her father to make her a widow with all due haste.

"We are on my land and in a fortified castle. My army is far more numerous than your father's current retinue. He knows that. He'll not engage in a battle he knows he cannot win."

She dropped her gaze to her horse's white mane, desperate to look at anything other than the man beside her. He had confused her for days now, and that confusion was only growing worse. "You're far more trusting of my father than I am."

"Time will tell," he replied. "In the meanwhile, welcome to your home."

Elizabeth lifted her gaze to look at the castle around her as they slowly proceeded through the outer bailey. Stables occupied one full length of the outer courtyard along with the animal pens, smokehouse, smithy, salt house, falcon mews, and guardhouse. Lights shone behind the shutters. At their approach, the windows swung open and curious onlookers followed their movements.

The inner courtyard was smaller with the kitchen, laundry, barracks, and servants' quarters taking up much of the outer walls. An entrance to the main living quarters within the castle stood open as though anticipating their arrival. A heartbeat later, Elizabeth could hear the excited murmur of voices as they came to an abrupt stop. Men and women spilled out the doors, coming to greet their laird and his new wife.

Two servants rushed up to gather the reins of their horses while Lachlan slipped from the saddle and came to her side. He reached up, assisting her down. As her feet hit the ground, she swayed ever so slightly. Lachlan must have noticed because he kept his hands at her waist while she steadied herself.

"Lachlan! You've returned." A tall man who looked almost as though he could be her husband's twin rushed forward to greet them. A woman with brown hair and an eager smile followed at his side.

"Reid? Lucy?" A smile transformed Lachlan's face. "I didn't expect you to be here when you could not come to the wedding. Did Quinn and Vivian have their baby?"

"Vivian had twins two days ago," Reid said with a grin. "The day you were married to Elizabeth. That must be a good omen if there ever was one."

"Twins?" Lachlan's eyes went wide.

Lucy nodded. "A boy who looks very much like Quinn, and a girl with fiery-red hair just like Vivian. They are called Alexander and Lilian."

Lachlan's concern deepened, etching fine lines around his eyes and mouth. "Was that why Vivian's labor was so hard, and why they sent for you?"

"Aye. Quinn was worried he might lose the very thing that has given his life meaning. He needed his own twin at his side to help steady him." Reid offered Lachlan an apologetic smile. "I'm so sorry we missed your wedding."

Lachlan shrugged. "One wedding is like any other."

Reid and Lucy shared a glance.

"Speaking of your lovely bride," Lucy said, stepping forward and pulling Elizabeth into an embrace. "You must be Elizabeth."

"Elizabeth, meet my cousins, Reid and Lucy." Reid was tall and lean, just like Lachlan, and they had the same intense blue eyes. Lucy was a firebrand of a woman whose head barely reached her husband's chin, but whose hug nearly lifted Elizabeth off her feet.

"I am pleased to make your acquaintance," Elizabeth replied.

Reid grinned. "Come, dear cousin-in-law, we are not so formal as all that." So saying, he gathered her into his arms and twirled her around once, with enough speed that her skirt belled out in the wind.

Elizabeth's response was a gasp of surprise that slipped into laughter. When he set her back on her feet, she wobbled slightly, but steadied herself. "Thank you both for such a kind welcome. I will admit to being slightly terrified to be among so many Douglases." She regretted the words the moment she uttered them.

Reid appeared not to have taken offense at her statement, but Lachlan's features darkened once more as he said, "We are not Douglases or Ruthvens here. Only people joined in a common purpose to live the lives we were destined for."

Fresh shivers of apprehension moved through Elizabeth. That was what she was worried about: what was she destined for? At the beginning of their journey her purpose had seemed so clear, but no longer.

"As happy as we are that you've returned to your home, Lachlan, you have other, more important things to contend with," Reid said.

"Such as?"

"If you would but look at your wife, you might have noticed how tired she is."

Lachlan's gaze intensified on her face.

"I'm not tired," she objected, then changed her mind. "Well, perhaps a little." She swayed on her feet once more.

Lachlan stepped past his cousins. "Why didn't you say something?" His hand was on her elbow, propelling her inside the castle and up the grand staircase. "We could have stopped to let you rest."

"You said you were in a hurry to reach Whittingehame."

"I was, but not by way of your demise. Stop being so obliging." Lachlan escorted her down a long hallway. At the end, he stopped and threw open a door, ushering her into the large chamber. "Lie down."

When still she didn't at once step toward the large, heavily canopied bed in the center of the room, he swooped her into his arms and settled her upon its surface. "I have neither the patience if you become ill, nor the time to tend you as your nursemaid. Rest. Agreed?"

The ghost of a smile came to her lips at the thought of this warrior tending her in the sickroom. He was so big and full of life. She had a hard time imagining him as anything but filled with energy and vitality as he was now. "If you insist."

"I do."

The door shut behind him before she could reply.

She gazed at the door for a long time. As the new mistress of the castle, she should be preparing to meet her staff and to start assisting in the daily needs of those under Lachlan's protection. Yet she yawned, and settled her cheek on the pillow, then closed her eyes. Perhaps just a few moments of rest would rid her of her soreness and help her stop thinking about the gentleness Lachlan had used when he'd lifted her into his arms just now.

LACHLAN FOUND REID and Lucy in the great hall. He still wasn't used to the idea that this ancient castle belonged entirely to him. He'd only lived there for three weeks, since the king and queen had given it to him as part of his marriage agreement. It still felt a little odd when he stepped up to the seats by the hearth where his cousins waited and he took the biggest chair—the laird's chair.

Reid's keen blue eyes studied him intently. "Dare I ask

how things are proceeding between you and your lovely wife?"

"As well as can be expected."

Reid frowned. "Is something amiss?"

"Elizabeth's father and a retinue of approximately fifteen men are following us. I expect them to arrive here by mid-afternoon tomorrow."

Reid stood, suddenly tense. "Will he and his men be sharpening their *clai'mors* and preparing for battle?"

"Sit down, Cousin. Settle yourself," Lachlan said in a weary voice, suddenly realizing how hard the journey to Whittingehame had been on him as well. He'd been on high alert the entire way, searching for dangers in the shadows. "Donald Ruthven is a brute, but he's no fool. He knows an attack on us would unite the lowland clans against him now that the king has tried to forge a truce."

Reid sat, but continued to scowl. "A prudent man might consider striking his enemy down first before he can stab him in the back."

"That man is my wife's father, which makes fighting him all the more complicated now." Lachlan shook his head. "I must be a man of peace in this situation—a diplomat, not a fighter." He sighed. "The last thing we all want right now is another full-out war between the clans. King James has stirred up enough trouble as it is with his witch trials."

"You are right. The days where I thought I could take on the world single-handedly are over." Reid reached for Lucy's hand and gave it an affectionate squeeze. "I am waging my battles differently now that my heart is engaged elsewhere."

Lucy's radiant smile was evidence enough that the married couple before him were truly happy and finding a way past their own troubles. If they could do such a thing, perhaps there was hope for Elizabeth and himself.

"What will you do when Donald Ruthven arrives?" Lucy asked, dragging her gaze away from the man at her side.

Lachlan allowed a wry smile to twist his lips. "I have no other option but to talk with the man."

"Are your men here prepared in case things do not go as planned?"

"Aye," Lachlan said. "I must thank you for sending Peter Grayden from your retinue to mine. He has proved himself beyond valuable as my Captain of the Guard. We had three weeks to prepare before my marriage to Elizabeth, and he has worked wonders with the men. They are trained and ready for whatever challenges may arise."

"Reid and I will try to think of all contingencies that could occur," Lucy added.

Lachlan nodded. Where Donald Ruthven was concerned, anything was possible—and none of it good.

CHAPTER NINE

ELIZABETH SLEPT FOR twelve hours straight, waking as the late morning sun shone so brightly into the room, she could no longer ignore its pull against her eyelids. For a peaceful moment all was well until she opened her eyes and glanced at the pale blue canopy overhead, then to the pale gold walls of the chamber Lachlan had led her to yesterday.

She bolted upright in bed and searched the room for her husband with her heart pounding in her ears. He was nowhere in sight and the space next to her remained undisturbed. Where had he slept? His kinsmen would have expected him to sleep beside her. Or had he been unable to rest at the thought of her father's imminent arrival?

Lachlan seemed to think a negotiation between the two of them could work. Elizabeth wasn't so certain. Her father was a hard man, and if she were honest, more in line with the lies he had always told her about their rival clan than the Douglases she'd met so far had proven to be. It was becoming harder and harder to believe the worst about the man she had married or his clan.

The more time she and Lachlan were together, the more

confused she became until it felt as though she continually floundered in a sea of self-doubt. How would she learn the truth? Or did she truly want to?

Heat rose to her cheeks as her thoughts turned back to the odd stirrings that warmed her when Lachlan had cradled her in his arms last night. She had never felt such things when Roland had touched her. The two men were total opposites. Roland was polished, polite, and proper. Lachlan had shown her he was caring, yet adventurous, slightly reckless, but definitely powerful and enigmatic. She could picture him setting her on the bed as he had last night, then falling back onto the feather bolster with her in his arms, making them both wildly happy and sated in the process.

She buried her face in her hands at the thought. How could she dare to think such a thing—to allow her imagination to take her places where she could not willingly go?

"Good afternoon."

Elizabeth looked up to see Lachlan's body filling the doorway of the bedchamber with a small tray balanced in his hands. She'd been so absorbed in her own thoughts she hadn't heard him enter.

He was fully dressed in buff-colored breeches and a plain white shirt embellished with only a simple white scarf at his neck. His hair was swept back from a face that was clean shaven. "I thought you might be hungry since you slept clear though dinner and breakfast."

Her stomach answered for her with a noisy growl. "I am

rather hungry," she admitted. "But I also feel gritty with the dirt from our travels still upon me."

"A bath is coming. But you should eat something first. You were quite weary when we arrived."

"You should have awakened me sooner. What must your staff think of me, sleeping the day away?"

He shrugged as he set the tray of tea and a scone with butter and jam beside her. "They are undoubtedly thinking you have endured much during your travels here. And while they are eager to meet you, they want that time to come when you are feeling at your best so you might be more pleased with them."

Her eyes widened. "They care whether or not I like them?"

"Of course, Elizabeth. These are your people now. They want their mistress to look upon them with favor." His gaze lingered on the soft swell of her breasts as they rose above her bodice before shifting to the length of her hair that spilled over her shoulders in a wild tangle, still mussed from her sleep. She brought up a hand, trying to tame it, but at another grumble from her stomach, she reached for the scone instead and took a bite.

"If you'd like something more substantial, I am certain Mistress Barron, our chatelaine, would be pleased to bring it to you."

Heat rushed to her cheeks once more. "I am not so fragile that I need to be fed in bed. I do not want anyone to fuss over me." It would make her feel even more guilty than she already felt about sleeping so long. She shifted her legs to the side of the bed as she took another bite of her scone, intending to start her day, when a shuffling sound came from the doorway.

"Here is Mistress Barron and her serving girls now with a bath and heated water." The women offered Elizabeth awkward curtsies as they carried their heavy pails over to the coals that still glowed in the fireplace. Once the tub was set, they emptied the water into the bath while Mistress Barron added more wood to the fire.

Elizabeth finished her scone and poured herself a cup of tea, sipping it in the silence that had descended over the chamber until the women bowed their way out, closing the door behind them. Once they were gone, she set the cup down and stood.

"I should leave you alone to bathe. When you are ready, come downstairs. I have several activities planned for us outside the castle today."

"What about my father? Shouldn't he be arriving today? Is it safe to be anywhere but inside these walls?"

"My men have not yet spotted him or his men in the distance and, as I told you yesterday, from Whittingehame you can see for miles in all directions."

Silence came over the room and she didn't know how to break the charged stiffness. He was different today. He seemed more at peace here at his home, and an easy camaraderie had fallen between them since before they had boarded the ship across the Firth. And yet, some of that earlier tension was back.

"Are you worried about my father's arrival?"

"The man seems intent on continuing the feud between our families. It's taken knowing you to reconcile my hatred of your clan. I'm ready for peace. But peace is only possible if both parties choose to lay down their swords." Lachlan issued a weary sigh. "If only he would meet me halfway. Your future—our future—is at stake if he doesn't."

Hot color flooded her cheeks and her chest suddenly tightened. "My father is a bit hot-headed. Perhaps I can—"

"Thank you for your offer, but I don't want to put you in harm's way. I will appeal to your father's sense of honor. The man must want his daughter to live in peace. I've negotiated several difficult agreements between the kingdom and other clans. Perhaps your father will come to his senses when he is presented with the facts about what continuing this feud will do to you." Lachlan offered her a lopsided smile and took a step closer, then, taking her hand, lifted it to his lips and kissed it. He looked down at her hand and hesitated a moment as he noted the pearl ring she always wore on her right hand. "Your ring, it is quite unusual."

"It was given to me by my father after my mother died so that I might have something to remember her by."

"'Tis beautiful. Just like the woman who wears it." She gazed at him wordlessly as he turned her hand over and lingeringly pressed his warm lips to her palm. The sensations darting through her were intimate, tender, and nothing like she'd ever felt before.

Slowly he lifted her palm to his cheek. "I want you to stay with me, Elizabeth. To be my wife, but only if that is what will please you as well." He held her gaze. In his eyes she saw not a hardened warrior, but a vulnerable man who was reaching out to her for what he wanted. But what he wanted was something she still wasn't ready to give. At her hesitation, his lids came down to veil his eyes. He kissed her palm again before releasing her.

She stared after him as he walked to the door. He paused, looking back as if he might say something more, but then he was gone and the door closed behind him. She stared at the wooden portal, willing it to open again and for him to return and follow through with what his eyes had exposed to her. But he did not.

All through her life she'd believed every word her clan had told her about the Douglases, blindly and without question. But many of the atrocities she'd been told about, if not all, might very well have been lies fabricated to propagate hatred between the two clans. And her father was on his way to continue that battle.

She knew, even though she and her father had never discussed it, that he had intended to capture Lachlan along their journey to Whittingehame Castle and murder him, then take her back into the Ruthven fold. But she and Lachlan had foiled attempts not once, but twice with their alternative travel plans.

Now that they'd arrived at Whittingehame, her father dared not kill the man in his own home. Besides, she would never allow him to succeed. Not anymore—and not just because of the blood oath between herself and Lachlan. Even though she still didn't fully trust Lachlan, she cared what happened to the man who was her husband.

As his wife, she belonged to him. She was his property, no matter how much the idea rankled. Her father no longer had any say in her life. He had to know that. So, what did he hope to accomplish by arriving on Lachlan's doorstep? Knowing her father, it would not be something good. They would know his intent soon enough.

Elizabeth released a pent-up breath as she forced her thoughts in a different direction. Lachlan wanted to spend time with her today. The very idea sent her pulse racing. She found herself dressing with particular care in her finest light green gown. The dress had seen better days, but it fit her well. Her father had never been one to spend on extravagances such as clothing for his only daughter. He always told her if someone wanted to take her to wife, they would take her as she was—with a meager dowry and no trousseau—or they would not take her at all.

As she made her way belowstairs, her thoughts turned to Lachlan. He hadn't taken her to wife for no gain, for he'd told her himself that he had been given this castle, a living, and four white horses by the king and queen. But he had asked nothing from her father.

Elizabeth continued past the landing until she could see Lachlan waited for her in the entry hall at the bottom of the stairs. He offered her a graceful bow. In one hand, he held the Bible they had been given as a wedding gift by the king and queen. He held out his other hand to her and said, "Come with me. I want to show you a special place."

She looked around her. "Where are Lucy and Reid?"

"They have decided to give us some privacy today. Ready?"

She took his hand and he guided her through the great hall and into the solar. They stopped just inside the doorway and he pulled his fingers from hers. "This room is now yours to do with as you please."

She turned to him. "But the solar is typically reserved for the laird and his business."

"I moved my desk out to be near the hearth in the great hall. I want you to have this room and all it contains."

A carpet in a patterned shade of beige, ivory, and red covered the stone floor and two beautiful tapestries with scenes of the Scottish countryside covered the walls. On one wall stood a large wooden bookcase loaded with books. Elizabeth's heart leapt at the idea of filling her days with reading. "There are so many books."

"Some of them I purchased. Some were spoils of war. All of them Reid brought with him, as I was storing them at his castle until I had a place of my own. I've been collecting them for years." He shrugged and stepped more fully inside, inviting her to do the same. "Among the collection is *The History of the Kings of Britain* by Geoffrey of Monmouth, featuring the popular characters of Arthur and Merlin, as well as Geoffrey Chaucer's *Canterbury Tales*." He held the Bible out to her. "I thought perhaps we could add this book to our library."

She hugged the Bible to her chest as she noted the two massive cream-covered chairs with matching footrests near the fireplace and a long bench opposite that. She could imagine herself curled up in a chair with her feet tucked beneath her, reading for hours on end, but such a thing could never happen. "'Tis truly a wonderful gesture, giving me this chamber, but I cannot accept. It would be a break in tradition."

"I want to break tradition. I do believe that is what you and I are all about—transforming what has always gone before us," Lachlan said as he sat in one of the oversized chairs and rested his head on the cushioned back. "And in further breaking the way things have always been, I'd rather have you in a room next to me during the day and in the midst of all the castle's business than tucked away on the third floor in relative isolation. You must accept this room. I insist."

Poignant emotion tightened her throat, making speech impossible so she nodded instead.

"Good. Now, where should we place the Bible? Somewhere all can see and where you can help the servants to read from it."

"You wish me to teach the servants to read?"

"Aye. I want them to be able to read from the Bible. If they can, they will all be safer from the witch hunters, should they come this way."

"You really care about your people."

"I care about their future, aye. We have terrible problems in our country that go beyond poverty and illness. During the past year I have watched both of my cousins' wives suffer most horribly because of the fanatical zeal of some who see witches everywhere and in every act of goodness or malice." He paused, looking earnestly into her face. "Will you teach them to read, Elizabeth?"

She nodded. "I will not only teach them to read but to write as well." His smiled warmed her clear to her toes. "When should we start?"

"Tomorrow morning, after chapel?"

She nodded. "I will need several slates and chalk."

"I will make certain you have what you need." He stood. "Now all that is settled, I have another surprise for you." He reached for her hand.

She hesitated. "Truly, you have gifted me far too much already with this chamber and a direction for my new life here."

After giving her hand a squeeze of encouragement, he

guided her from the room. "'Tis market day in Whittinge-hame village. I have it on good authority the draper is there with many lengths of beautiful silks and brocades, and that the town seamstress is more than eager to make her new mistress several new gowns all in the latest styles."

"I couldn't possibly impose—"

"Nonsense," Lachlan said, guiding her out of the castle to where two horses waited. "I intend to give you not only what you need, but also what you desire." He lifted her onto the horse's back. His hands lingered at her waist. She closed her eyes, reveling in the sensations of his hands on her body. With each day, and each touch, her capitulation threatened as he wore her down with his strength and his passion.

"Elizabeth?"

She opened her eyes slowly, and when she did her breath caught at what she saw on his face. His eyes filled with wonder and his smile was blatantly sensual. "Why are you being so considerate? You need not. I belong to you."

"You matter to me."

Four simple words. Wild color stained her cheeks as she looked down at his hands, which still encircled her waist. "You are starting to matter to me as well."

Heaven help them both.

LACHLAN HAD SENT their marketing home with one of the

servants who attended them, while he and Elizabeth went another direction, to a place he had only discovered the week before near the glen.

"Where are you taking me?" she asked from atop her horse.

"To a special place. It's only a little farther."

She frowned as she looked at the darkening sky. "It's dusk. The night is upon us."

He knew she was thinking of her father. Lachlan's thoughts had also strayed in that direction a time or two during the day. He had expected Donald Ruthven to show himself at Whittingehame by now, yet he had not. Part of Lachlan wondered why, but the other part dismissed the man entirely. He had decided long ago not to give the Ruthvens any more of his thoughts than they deserved.

And the woman before him? Did he no longer see her as a Ruthven? Forcing the question away, he turned to Elizabeth. "I do not fear your father. Please, trust me. All will be well." At least that was his hope.

As he rode beside her in silence, he noted that her shoulders were no longer as tense, and the lines around her eyes had eased in the past two days. Was it his own hopeful imagination, or was Elizabeth softening toward him?

After a few moments more, he reined his horse to a stop. "We have arrived." The only movement in the night was the wind as it rustled through the leaves overhead.

She stopped beside him. He slipped from his horse's

back and then helped her dismount. He tethered the animals to a nearby gorse bush with enough lead so they could graze, before removing a blanket from the saddlebag. He offered Elizabeth his hand. She took it and together they set off to a clearing ahead.

She smiled and something in her face changed. Her eyes lifted to his, filled with an emotion he'd never seen there before. One she'd never let him see as fully as she did now. Was it acceptance, friendship, or something more? They might already be married to each other, but they still had a long way to go to build a life together. How did two people whose lives up to this point had been filled with trauma and pain find a way to each other when everything around them conspired against them?

He came to a stop in a meadow a few yards away from the horses. Dropping her hand, he spread the blanket on the ground. "Come, join me," he said, stretching atop the blanket. "I have one more gift to give to you."

"Nay," she protested as she settled beside him. "You have already given me too much."

"It is a gift that has already been bestowed on us both." He propped himself up on his elbow, gazing at her. "I know it disturbs you to think of me as a Douglas, and if I am truly honest with you, I flinch inside when I hear your Ruthven name. Both of our pasts are filled with violence and hatred of one clan toward the other. But you and I no longer have to claim those names."

"But those are our names."

"Nay. When the king gave me this castle as part of your dowry, he also bestowed upon us both a title: I am the Earl of March and you the Countess of March. We can make it be known that we prefer to use our titles instead of our clan names. Would that be acceptable by you?" He reached for her hand, held it in his own with uncertain fingers, afraid suddenly of what her answer might be.

"Aye," she replied with a catch in her voice. "That is the kindest thing anyone has ever done for me. I accept, Laird March."

"I am pleased, Countess March."

A moment later her eyes filled with a question. "Was the grass in the meadow what you wanted to show me?"

With a quick smile, he lay back down on the blanket and pointed to the sky that had faded into black. "Behold, the stars."

"I've seen stars before," she said a moment before she gasped. "Oh my, they were never as sharply defined against the night sky as this." She shifted her body toward his until she was settled against his side. "You're trembling," she whispered, sounding surprised.

"You do that to me."

She tightened her fingers around his and scooted closer.

Warmed by the feel of her body against his, he stared not at the sky but at her. A soft breeze continued to tousle Elizabeth's hair as she searched the star-blazed sky. Thousands of stars glittered like diamonds overhead. "The Greeks called that swath of orange and gold above us the Milky Circle."

"Where did you learn about the stars?"

"From my father. He taught me about astronomy. After he and mother were gone, I spent much of my early life alone. But wherever I looked up at the night sky I could always imagine them watching down over me." He paused. "I've never told anyone that before."

"Thank you for sharing that with me. It couldn't have been easy." She said nothing more, but he knew where her thoughts went. It was because of her clan that he had been so alone.

He drew in her fragrance as he reveled in her closeness. "If you are interested in learning more about the night sky, there is a book in the library that might interest you, *On the Revolutions of the Heavenly Spheres* by Nicolaus Copernicus. He theorized that the center of our universe is the sun and not the Earth, as scientists have thought."

"I'd like to read that book." Her eyes appeared luminescent as the stars danced in their depths.

Wrapped in silence, they watched the stars glitter in the sky and as they did, Lachlan realized tonight Elizabeth had given him a gift as well. She had given him back his dreams. While the entirety of his life had been filled with one battle after another, he'd had to suppress any hopes for the future. And when he did allow himself to imagine the future, half the time he didn't think he deserved for his dreams to become reality, the other half he was terrified they'd be stolen away, and he was too afraid of the pain.

Yet at Elizabeth's side tonight, anything seemed possible, even those things he'd never allowed himself to want. A wife. A family. A future.

She turned to him and her eyes searched his briefly. To his surprise she stretched over him and lightly kissed him on the lips.

He responded, touched by her sweetness, her warmth.

When they came apart a moment later, she pulled back with a smile. "We should make our way back to the castle. You might not fear my father, but I do." Her eyes became troubled. "I do not understand why he is taking so long to arrive."

Lachlan stood, then helped her up. "Perhaps he has changed his mind and will leave things as they are."

"Perhaps." The word was barely a whisper.

He folded the blanket and tucked it under his arm. When he was done, he took her hand once more in his own, and hand-in-hand they walked slowly back to the horses. Lachlan smiled into the darkness as he set Elizabeth atop her horse. Even though he hadn't thought of Elizabeth in a favorable way at the time of their marriage, the king and queen had done him a greater service than he'd ever imagined. His enemy had become his friend, and with luck they would become a lot more in the days and weeks ahead.

If only he could win her father over as easily.

Chapter Ten

THE FIRST DRESS arrived the next morning. It was an exquisite pale yellow silk gown with clean lines that fit Elizabeth's body to perfection. Gold braid had been added to the bodice and sleeves and accented with tiny seed pearls. It was the most sumptuous dress she had ever owned, and she wore it now in the solar as she finished her first lesson with twelve of the castle's servants—four women and eight men. Mistress Barron and Peter Grayden were among them.

For two hours they had practiced the alphabet, and by the end of their time together all twelve had learned to write their names. Pride filled Elizabeth as she accepted Mistress Barron's slate with her name spelled properly upon the gray-green sheet of stone. "You did well today."

She curtsied as she said, "As long as I can remember, I've always wanted tae learn how tae read and write. 'Tis truly more than I ever dreamed possible. Thank ye, milady."

Elizabeth knew exactly how the chatelaine felt. In the past few days, her own life had taken an unforeseen turn. She was now mistress of her own home, and she'd been given a purpose that went far beyond herself. The castle residents were eager to sit at her feet and soak up whatever she would give them in order to better their own lives.

Just as Lachlan had bettered hers. He had changed. Or was it she who had become something different, molded by her circumstances? When she was in Lachlan's presence, she no longer felt a twist of hatred. Instead, when he looked her way and smiled, her stomach took flight in the most disturbing of ways. And when he touched her . . . an odd warmth flowed through her limbs. A wild cascade of sensations tumbled through Elizabeth as she remembered how Lachlan had taken her hand as they walked through the village yesterday, and how he had pulled her against the hard musculature of his chest when she'd started to trip on an uneven cobblestone.

"How did the lessons go?" a voice called from the doorway.

Elizabeth was jarred from her thoughts at the sight of Lucy coming into the chamber. "Better than I could ever have expected. They are all so eager to learn."

Lucy sat on the bench, and put out a beckoning hand to Elizabeth. "They are fortunate you can teach them such skills."

"I feel like I am the fortunate one."

"The Douglas men are unique among men," Lucy said with an understanding smile. "I just sent a servant off to deliver a letter from Lachlan to my sister-in-law, Vivian, asking her to take on a new student, training her in the art of healing. For a Jane Wenham? Do you know her?"

"Aye. Lachlan and I met her on our travels here." Elizabeth had felt a bond with Lucy from the moment they had met. She was so easy to talk to. Thrilled that she had come to her now, Elizabeth set the slate she held on a table, then moved to sit beside her new cousin. She'd had several intimate conversations with the queen while she'd been at Falkland Palace, but it had been years before that since she'd enjoyed female companionship. And never had she talked with another woman about a man. "Can I ask you something?"

Lucy settled her hands in her lap. "Anything."

"I know you had little choice in your marriage partner, much like myself. Did you always like Reid?"

Lucy's smile turned soft. "I did, but I tried to convince myself I did not. It was easier to hold myself apart than to trust him." Her gaze sharpened. "Do you ask because of your desire to know more about me and Reid, or does the question have more to do with you and Lachlan?"

"Is it that easy to see through my words?"

"It is more of what is in your expression than what is in your words," Lucy replied. "Is all going well between you two?"

"Apart from the fact he is insufferable at times."

Lucy smiled and her eyes danced. "You like him."

"The way I feel matters not. My father is coming, and he is set upon revenge. The feud between our families has gone on too long for my marriage to a Douglas to make any difference to him. Now that he's gotten what he wanted from the king, my father will find a way to stir up trouble again."

"Don't let him. Stand for what you want, regardless of what has passed between the clans before now."

Elizabeth frowned. "I've never gone against my father before."

"What will be the result if you don't?"

Her heart gave a jerk and then began to pound wildly. "A battle."

"If it comes to that, then people will die on both sides of that conflict. Is that what you want?"

Elizabeth stood. "I don't know what I want," she said, her voice shaking. "This would be so much easier if I did."

"You do know what you want," Lucy said smoothly. "You are simply afraid to reach for it."

"I'm not as brave as you."

"Aye, you are. You've already proven that a hundred times in the last few days. It takes a strong and brave woman to leave everyone and everything she knows behind and to start over with no guarantees or promises."

But Lachlan had made her one promise: to keep her from harm. But in keeping that promise, would he endanger himself instead? Could she put an end to it all by standing up to her father?

Elizabeth's thoughts were an incoherent jumble as her

emotions vacillated between hope, anxiety, and fear. "You do not know my father."

Lucy raised a brow. "And he knows not the woman you mean to become." She stood. "If you truly care about his welfare and the lives of the people in this castle, then you'll stand up to him and fast."

"Why do you say that?" Panic speared through Elizabeth.

"Because your father and his men were spotted approaching the castle over two hours ago. They will be here at any moment."

Elizabeth met Lucy's gaze. "Why did you not say something sooner?"

"Because ten minutes ago you were not ready for an encounter with your father. Now you are not only prepared, you are primed for battle."

"I'm not so certain of that," Elizabeth admitted, feeling suddenly heavy. "He hasn't arrived yet?"

Lucy shook her head. "Not as of ten minutes ago."

"Where's Lachlan? I must speak with him."

"In the great hall with Reid, waiting."

Elizabeth didn't hesitate, she hastened through the doorway of the solar that emptied into the great hall. "Lachlan. I must speak with you. 'Tis urgent—" She skidded to a stop. "Father." Elizabeth was so surprised to see her father standing before her she could do little more than gasp and stare. When she recovered some of her equilibrium she said, "You are already here."

Only her father and the young man, Keddy, whom her father had taken under his wing, were present from their clan. Yet six other men stood nearby, waiting and watching.

"Lady Elizabeth Douglas." Keddy's lips pulled up at the corners and his eyes glittered with malice.

"The Countess of March," Lachlan corrected.

"I've come to take you home, Lizzie," her father said.

"Nay." Her heart was pounding like a drum in her chest, and her hands were shaking so badly she balled them into fists at her sides. Her gaze moved beyond her father not to his warriors but to the five older men dressed in their Sunday best. Another man, a minister—dressed in a black robe with a white collar—hugged a parchment scroll to his chest. The look in his eyes was not one of welcome, but a portent that something horrible was about to transpire. When her gaze shifted back to her father, a dangerous smile pulled up the edges of his hard mouth. It was a smile like none she'd ever seen before.

Behind the men stood Reid, Peter Grayden, and Mistress Barron, as well as several of the other servants who had been her students only a few minutes ago. The tension in the chamber was thick, but fury burned away the despair numbing her emotions. "I will not go with you. This is my home."

"Not for long."

"I've had enough of your blustering, Ruthven. State your purpose." Lachlan's features were as hard as stone. "I invited you in so we might negotiate beyond what the king and queen have already done. I'd hoped we might finally put this battle between our two clans to rest, as they wanted."

"We'll put the matter to rest all right." Donald Ruthven laughed as his eyes glinted like the amber flames of a fire. "And there will be no bloodshed but yours."

Elizabeth felt a chill touch her spine as a commotion came from the doorway. The castle's warriors suddenly filled the great hall. Their swords were present, but not drawn as they formed a half circle around her father and the other men. "What is this, Father? What are you doing?" Elizabeth asked when the noise settled.

"Battling evil." The very callousness of her father's tone made her heart leap in fear.

"There is no evil here." Her voice was hoarse and oddly broken.

"Oh, but there is, my girl. There is so much evil that you can no longer see clearly through the shadows it casts over you."

On one side of her, Elizabeth could feel waves of rage rush toward her father and yet Lachlan contained his emotions. She could see the cost to him in the leaping of his pulse at his temple, in the clenching of his jaw, and the coiled tension of his muscles.

On the other side of her, her father smiled craftily, perfectly relaxed. Which was odd. What was he about? Why didn't he just say what he'd come to say? Because he not only wanted to threaten Lachlan, he also wanted him to suffer.

When she could bear no more, she asked, "If you have something to say, Father, say it."

"There are witches and warlocks in this land, my girl. We are in a battle to save not only ourselves but the very heart of Scotland. We have a responsibility to keep witches and warlocks from roaming freely about this great land of ours, which is why I have come to accuse your husband, Lachlan Douglas, of being a warlock, in league with the Devil to turn you against your own family." Her father grabbed her arm in an attempt to pull her toward him.

Elizabeth recoiled from his touch as his words landed with the force of thunder. Up until that moment she had always assumed her father was a strict but honorable man, but suddenly, before her eyes it was as if a veil had been dropped and she no longer saw the brave, brawny warrior. In his place stood an ambitious, ruthless man, who had no pleasant mask to hide his inner ugliness now. "Nay, Father. I will not let you do this. Lachlan is no warlock."

"The evidence against him says he is." Donald Ruthven bared his teeth.

The whisper of steel sounded all around them as Reid and the other warriors drew their swords. But Lachlan stayed the weapons with a tight shake of his head.

"If you have such evidence, then put it forward," Lachlan said grimly. "For I know I have no evil upon my soul."

"Liar!" Keddy erupted as his gaze moved past Lachlan to somewhere behind him. "Begone, you wretched spirit!" He pointed with one finger to something behind Lachlan. "The Devil is in the air. I can see him prancing about this pretender as if he's on a stage. The Devil whispers to him as he stands beside him now, directing him what to say and what to do." Keddy spun toward the others in the chamber. "Do you not see the Devil in our midst?"

"There is nothing there," Elizabeth cried out even as she clutched Lachlan's arm to keep herself upright as the room swam before her eyes. Would her father really stoop so low as to charge Lachlan with witchcraft in order to wrest him away from her? Those who were arrested, questioned, and then charged were more often than not burned at the stake with very little effort made to seek their innocence.

"Again, I ask, what evidence have you?" Lachlan challenged.

Her father pushed the minister forward. "This man of God will be only too happy to relay what evils you have wrought on your journey to this castle with my innocent daughter. The elders are here as witnesses."

The minister cleared his throat as he unrolled a parchment scroll. "Lachlan Douglas, I have a warrant for your arrest. You are charged with multiple counts of sorcery. The charges are as follows: You gave a potion to Bessie Broun at the Buckhaven Inn that sent her into convulsions, as though she herself was possessed by demons. There are witnesses who heard you use magical chants to calm her. Other witnesses claimed you nearly sacrificed your own wife in your marriage bed while at Ravenscraig Castle. We have the blood-soaked linens as proof of the tale." The minister's gaze shifted to Elizabeth. "'Tis glad I am you survived that trauma, child."

"Nay!" Elizabeth protested. "You are wrong. I—"

"Leave it be, Elizabeth," Lachlan interrupted. A warning flashed through his eyes. He did not want her to say anything that might implicate her.

But she could not hold her tongue entirely. "He is not a warlock. I know this!"

The minister's accusing gaze moved back to Lachlan as he continued. "On the Firth of Forth you caused the sea to churn and drowned Dillon Kemp, and you almost claimed the life of Thomas Cockburn. There are multiple witnesses who heard you call out an enchantment that capsized the small fishing vessel near your mighty ship."

Elizabeth listened, with a growing sense of unreality. All the charges they'd read so far were fabrications drawn from only parts of the actual truth.

"And finally," the minister droned on, "while in Aberlady at the Cairn Inn, you changed yourself into your familiar form—that of a black cat—as you escorted your wife to the inn to partake in a meal."

"Nay!" Elizabeth said with despair. "That was an actual barn cat. I was in the presence of both Lachlan and the cat at the same time."

The minister met her gaze. "The Devil is capable of

many things. I suspect appearing in two forms at once is but an easy task for one so powerful." He cleared his throat once more and straightened. He held out the order of arrest and read:

"In whereas the honorable Roland Carswell, Mistresses Bessie Broun, Jane and Meg Wenham, Mariam Swinton, and the crew of the fishing vessel *The Four Winds* have appeared before us and made significant complaints against Lachlan Douglas, the Earl of March, for suspicion of witchcraft, and injury done to Bessie Broun and Dillon Kemp, and contrary to the peace sought by our Sovereign rulers, James and Anne, King and Queen of Scotland, you are therefore required to turn yourself over to be examined and interviewed. Failure to comply will be at your own peril. Signed, Hugh Godfrey, in accordance with the Privy Council of Scotland on behalf of King James VI."

There was a collective intake of breath, and a low murmur that followed as those present talked among themselves. Reid stepped between the minister and Lachlan. "This cannot be. Lachlan Douglas is one of the king's favored warriors. The king would never seek his arrest."

"Unless the king believes the Earl of March truly is a warlock," one of the elders, a balding man with mottled cheeks, spoke for the group. "We have sent word to His Grace at Falkland. If he agrees you should be released, he will send word to us, I am certain. Until then, you are still required to submit yourself to us and our examination."

Reid turned and gripped both Lachlan's arms. "The men and I will clear the way for your escape. Leave here at once and go to Kinmount House with Quinn and Vivian. By royal decree, Kinmount is designated as a sanctuary for all who might be accused as a witch or a warlock. Even James cannot touch you there."

Lachlan stood tall as a bleak silence fell over the chamber. "I will not run from this. To do so would make me appear as though I am guilty. I am not." He turned toward Donald Ruthven. "This is a ploy by a dangerous man to try and subdue his enemy with the least effort possible."

"This is folly and conjecture," Reid added. "'Tis insulting that it is being taken seriously." Reid paced back and forth in front of Lachlan as he branded each elder with an angry glare. "You would not dare take him to the tribunal."

"Did you hear that?" her father asked. "I believe Reid Douglas just threatened the elders gathered here. Perhaps we can expand that arrest warrant to include Reid Douglas as well?"

"Nay, Reid," Lucy cried, coming to her husband's side. "You cannot help your cousin if you are also in gaol. Please, stand down."

Reid hesitated a moment, then released a harsh breath. "I will go to the king myself, with all due haste," he said to Lachlan.

The tallest of the elders drew a pair of iron manacles from a satchel he carried over his shoulder and held them out to Lachlan. "In the meanwhile, you must come with us."

Elizabeth looked up at her husband, her eyes filled with misery and disbelief. "What can I do? How can I help?"

Lachlan ignored the manacles as he took her icy hands in his. "Stay here. Be strong. I am a great believer in the truth."

"Where are you taking him?" Elizabeth asked.

"To the tolbooth in Haddington," the minister replied.

Elizabeth did not take her eyes from Lachlan while they secured the manacles around his wrists and snapped them tight before jerking him into motion toward the doorway and through a path created by his men. They were taking him to gaol.

Lachlan's eyes were wide, yet unseeing, staring past them all as if focusing instead on the horror he suspected was ahead. With every step, the chains that bound him rattled, the jarring, sound echoing deep in her soul.

CHAPTER ELEVEN

OBLIVIOUS TO THE chaos around her, Elizabeth paced as her thoughts spun. There was guilt—terrible, gut-wrenching guilt—that her father had done this to Lachlan. But there was also an emptiness she did not understand.

Her father's voice cut through the turmoil. "I'll teach you to say no to me. Get your things, Lizzie. We are leaving."

Elizabeth startled at the barely concealed outrage on her father's face. "I told you before and I'll tell you again, nay. I am no longer your concern."

He took her elbow. "You'll come with me or I'll carry you out of here, tied up if need be."

She twisted free, scorched by his touch. "Oh, nay," she exploded, her body shaking with wrath. "The only reason you wish me to leave this place is so you will have more leverage over the Douglases."

"Elizabeth," her father growled.

Elizabeth backed up, avoiding his reach. "I'm tired of not knowing what is truth and what is a lie. From now on, I only want the truth from you and everyone else."

"The truth is your husband is a warlock, and that he will be put to death. When he is gone, do you really want to remain here surrounded by the very people who hate and despise you?"

Determined to stand up not only for herself, but also for a man she believed was innocent, Elizabeth hurried from the great hall. She would not give in to the demands of her father or the sense of impending doom she'd been struggling to contain since she and Lachlan had taken their vows.

Her father chased after her. "Returning to the clan is the only possible solution to your problem," he called.

She wheeled around, confronting her father once more. "Don't you dare suggest the clan would be a refuge for me when it has always been more like a prison. Only once I left did I finally catch a glimpse of what my life might hold. And now you're trying to take that away from me as well."

"I've taken nothing from you, girl. But that bastard you call husband has."

Elizabeth narrowed her eyes. "Another lie, Father?"

"You decide," he said, his gaze fixed on her.

"I'm listening."

"You were only a young girl when your mother died, and I let you think her death was due to natural causes because you were mired in grief. But that is not the whole truth."

Her heart rose in her throat. "Go on."

"Lachlan Douglas blamed our clan for his parents' deaths. One night, when he was only a lad of seven, he infiltrated Ruthven Castle and entered my and your mother's bedchamber. Under the cover of the night, he cursed us both then fled before he could be apprehended. The next day your mother was dead. The wise woman said her heart simply stopped beating."

Elizabeth heard whimpers come from her own throat as the memory of holding her mother's lifeless body in her arms came back to her. She remembered stroking her mother's hair and rocking her gently, begging her to wake up. Yet she had not.

Another memory came to her just as suddenly—a memory she'd tucked deep inside—that of a young boy not coming into her parents' bedchamber, but her own. He hadn't been armed. He hadn't demanded anything. He'd simply stared at her with the most soulful eyes she had ever seen. Blue eyes. Lachlan's eyes.

Her father spoke the truth, at least in part. Lachlan had come to them. But why? Had he sought revenge; he could have taken it that night. Yet, she clearly remembered him with no weapon in his hands. But sorcery needed no blade. The spoken word—be it enchantment or curse—could have done just as much damage.

Nay! Elizabeth closed her eyes, breathing raggedly, as she struggled to push those memories away. Her father was trying to sow doubt in her mind, to make her fear the man she'd been forced to marry but had begun to trust.

She had to believe Lachlan was innocent. At least for

now. When she felt more in control, she opened her eyes, and despite the heaviness that weighed her down, she shook her head. "That doesn't prove anything. If you and Mother had been killed by the Douglases, I might have vented my anger in the same way."

Her father's face was colorless now, and pain reflected in his eyes. "'Twas a curse, I tell you."

Her fingernails dug into the palms of her hands as she tried to force the memories and her father's accusations away. "I don't believe you," she said before turning away and heading out the door. She needed to find someone to help her get to Haddington before the entire world threatened to turn upside down.

THAT NIGHT AND early into the following morning passed in darkness for Lachlan as he sat upon the cold stone floor with mice scurrying about his feet. Despite the fact it was summer, only cold seemed to seep through the thick stone walls of the tolbooth in Haddington. He'd been given a cell with a small window that looked out onto the main street. No doubt his position with the king was the reason why he had this indulgence. While his captors might fear his magical abilities, they feared retribution by the king more for abusing one of his warriors. Yet even so, the air in the cell was stale with the stench of decay.

Word must have reached the king by now, and yet Lachlan was still a prisoner. Were his accusers waiting for him to be weary from anxiety and exhaustion until they questioned him? He'd heard rumors of such tactics—keeping the prisoners awake, feeding them little, and then torturing them for hours on end in order to gain confessions, attesting to all manner of untrue sorcery and sin.

An hour later, when the sun finally cast a long shadow into his cell, Lachlan heard footsteps on the flagstone outside his door. A moment later a loud scraping sounded as the iron bolt slid back. The door creaked open, revealing a tall, lean man with dark hair and, if not kind, at least a friendly face. In his hands he held a tray, which he came forward with and set on the floor beside Lachlan. "Lachlan Douglas," he greeted. "I am the Lord Chancellor, John Maitland. I was sent by the king to make certain you were well tended."

Lachlan allowed hope to blossom. "I am to be released then."

At the Lord Chancellor's expression, any hope Lachlan held died.

"The king is intent upon ridding his kingdom of all evil. He has proclaimed he is appointed by God himself to accomplish that task, and will not rest until the deed is done. The Privy Council and the ministers of this great land have worked tirelessly to uncover the Devil's work and all those who wreak havoc on his behalf. Your arrest was necessary in order to demonstrate our commitment to seeing the king's orders executed. No one is above suspicion, whether they be laird, lady, or peasant."

Lachlan scoffed. "You make an example of an innocent man?"

"If you are innocent, that will come to light." The Lord Chancellor dropped his gaze. "Your interrogation will begin this afternoon. The king himself will be present at the proceedings. He means to handle your case with care so that other chieftains do not get the idea that they can settle clan disputes by accusing each other of witchcraft."

Lachlan tried to see that as a hopeful sign. If the king were present, there was less of a chance of Donald Ruthven abusing the process for his own purposes.

"He wishes to see that justice is served," the Lord Chancellor said as though reading Lachlan's thoughts.

"Thank you," Lachlan said. "As long as it is justice and not revenge that is served, I have no fear. I am an innocent man."

The Lord Chancellor looked at him with a mixture of sadness and admiration before he stepped back through the door, shut it, then slid the bolt tight.

THAT AFTERNOON, ONE of the guards opened the door and, keeping Lachlan's manacles on his wrists, led him outside the tolbooth to a transport cart. Four guards walked before the cart while another four followed behind, all with their swords drawn, prepared for any interference that might come their way.

The cart rattled through the small town until it stopped outside the ruins of Berwick's Old Parish church. "We're here," one of the guards announced as he helped Lachlan out of the cart before escorting him into the tribunal chamber.

Inside the building, the air was heavy with the smell of tallow from the multitude of candles burning in sconces on the walls of the chamber, as well as that of pitch and decay. It took Lachlan's eyes a moment to adjust to the bright light, but when they did, he saw King James himself striding back and forth across a raised dais at the front of the room. Every few steps, the king stopped and looked about the chamber as if expecting to find a witch among those in attendance.

Lachlan scanned the faces of those gathered until he found what he sought. Elizabeth stood on the left side of the chamber with Reid and Lucy at her side. His wife's face was pale and her features drawn as she clutched her hands in front of her with such force her knuckles had turned white. Her father and several other Ruthvens, including Keddy, stood closer to the front. Others he recognized in the chamber were Peter Grayden and several of his warriors, along with the minister, Hugh Godfrey, and the five elders who had arrested him. The remainder of the crowd were no doubt local residents who were curious to see if a laird could be punished as easily as any of them might be.

Silence fell over the chamber as he was ushered onto the dais to stand beside the king. King James's gaze fell on him, not with sympathy, but with a fierceness Lachlan had never witnessed before. "Your Grace," he greeted with a deep bow.

"I'm very angry with you," King James said through narrowed eyes. "Your cousin, Reid, was quite insistent that I come here myself and oversee these proceedings, forcing me to abandon my own pleasures."

"My apologies, Your Grace. This whole event is a farce, forced upon me by none other than Donald Ruthven."

The king's gaze connected with the Ruthven in question. "Aye, he might have started this whole thing, but there are serious charges against you that must be reconciled."

Lachlan's body tensed. "Your Grace, 'tis me, one of your warriors. You know me. You trust me, or at least you did once."

"'Tis more complicated than that. The Devil's clutch may be on you yet. We must prove otherwise."

Lachlan shivered as a chill walked his spine. "You know me, Your Grace."

"I cannot make an exception for even one man, whether I know him or not, if charges are brought against him." Beads of perspiration appeared on James's forehead as his gaze moved across the increasing crowd. After a long pause, he said, "The specter of the Devil stalks this land. I trust in these proceedings to let the truth be known."

"The truth is, I am innocent. I'm no sorcerer, but I am

your guardsman. 'Tis my duty and my honor to keep you safe as a Scot, a Stuart, and the rightful king. And in return, you had once vowed the same to me."

Color bloomed on James's cheeks even as his eyes narrowed. "You dare to judge me?"

"Nay, Your Grace," Lachlan replied, his jaw tense. "But it appears you are about to judge me."

James frowned but said nothing more as a tall, thin man wearing a white wig and a scarlet robe took his place on the dais. As he did, the murmur of the crowd died down until there was only silence. John Skene, the Lord Advocate, proceeded, saying in a voice loud enough for all to hear, "Lachlan Douglas, Earl of March, you have been brought before this tribunal to answer for the following crimes:

"Item: You have acted against King James VI's laws governing the use of sorcery.

"Item: You have used potions to cause sickness and enchantments to unbaptize and cause the Devil to take over Bessie Broun's soul.

"Item: You used enchantments to stir up the waters of the Firth of Forth causing the death of Dillon Kemp, and to incite willful acts of evil that nearly took the lives of five others.

"Item: By consorting with the Devil, you attempted to sacrifice your wife on the altar of matrimony.

"Item: You shapeshifted into a black cat and summoned up other spirits as you passed through the village of Aberlady.

"We have ample testimony from those who've been affected by your evil deeds, and yet I must ask, how do you plead to these charges?"

Anger surged inside Lachlan as he looked first to the king, then to Elizabeth. Both refused to meet his gaze as though they feared he might somehow influence their behavior. When his gaze lit on Donald Ruthven, the man's mouth twisted into a slow smile of satisfaction. "Not guilty," Lachlan replied.

The Lord Advocate frowned. "We have ample evidence against you."

"Then bring forth your 'proof,' and I will help you to see the actual truth," Lachlan said.

The minister who had arrested him stepped forward with a Bible in his hands. His cheeks were mottled and his eyes blazed. "Lachlan Douglas, what contract have you made with the Devil?"

"I've made no contract with the unclean one."

"He lies!" the minister shouted as the room suddenly became charged with both energy and noise.

"Silence," the Lord Advocate shouted over the murmurs of those gathered. "We will hear more testimony." He turned back to the minister. "If you have a point to make, make it, sir."

The minister held the book out to Lachlan. "Touch this holy book and let us see if your flesh doth burn."

Lachlan lifted a manacled hand, and with chains rattling, he placed his right hand atop the Bible. When nothing happened, Lachlan allowed himself a small smile of satisfaction.

"Look! He smiles!" Someone in the crowd shouted. "The Devil helps tae keep him from bursting into flames."

Lachlan startled. "What absurdity is this? The Devil is nowhere near me. I am but a man who touches and reads from the Bible every day."

"Then read a passage now," the minister said, shoving the Bible at him with a fanatical grin.

Lachlan took the holy book in his hands and flipped it open to a random page. He looked down at the words, and for a moment terror filled him as he saw that the book was not in the king's tongue, but in Latin. Lachlan struggled to control his breathing. He might not fluently speak the language, but he had studied it for years and knew many of the words. At least enough to pass this suddenly-thrust-upon-him test.

He'd opened the pages of Deuteronomy. His gaze immediately caught on the words "*confortare et esto robustus.*" He read the passage in Latin. "Be strong and courageous. Do not be afraid or terrified because of them, for the Lord your God goes with you; he will never leave you nor forsake you."

"How dare you speak the words of God!" the minister hissed as his hand cracked against Lachlan's cheek with brutal outrage. "What powers do you have that allow you to speak so?"

"I have no powers other than those given to a mortal man."

"The Devil is his Master." The minister's voice rose. "You are charged with witchcraft and sorcery."

Despite the panic that threatened, Lachlan kept his emotions in check. Echoing the man's anger would do nothing to help his cause. He needed to be rational and logical in his own defense since it appeared even the king would not stand for him. "I am innocent," he said again. "I have done no witchcraft or sorcery."

"I ask again, what contract have you made with the Devil?"

"None." Lachlan's heart pounded painfully in his chest.

"Enough, Godfrey!" A voice boomed above the others. "This line of questioning is getting us nowhere and is only inciting hysteria. How am I to fulfill my promise to God to root out witches from this kingdom when I am surrounded by fools?" the king asked.

Hugh Godfrey flinched at the insult before he schooled his features once more. "How would you like to proceed, Your Grace?"

"There are ways to hasten this man's confession, should he need to make one." The king stepped forward. His eyes locked upon Lachlan. "Do you tell us what we wish to know willingly, or shall we allow more forceful tests to loosen your tongue? I personally have no stomach for the devices, but they are very effective at bringing on a confession."

He spoke of torture. A shudder passed through Lachlan, but he kept his face impassive.

"There is another way," the Lord Advocate said as he took the Bible from Lachlan's hands and set it on the table behind him. "Since it is our quest to determine if this man should stand trial as a witch, if we had irrefutable proof, then a trial would be all but certain."

"What are you suggesting?" the king asked with a frown.

Hugh Godfrey's eyes glinted with excitement. "It is well known that to seal a pact with the Devil, the dark one will suck upon the flesh, leaving a mark, a spot, or a teat in some hidden place. When pricked with a needle, if the mark neither bleeds nor causes pain, then it is a true Devil's Mark. Such a mark can be easily mistaken for one that is naturally occurring upon the flesh, so only an expert in these matters might be trusted to find such a devious contract between a human and the dark one. John Swinton is here in Berwick. He is renowned for his skills as a pricker and has sent many witches to the flames. Shall I send for him?"

Lachlan tensed as he imagined the long, sharp needle they would thrust into his flesh and quite possibly over every inch of his body. Swinton might be highly regarded for his skill as a pricker, but he was also Mariam Swinton's—one of his accusers—father. Would the man be more thorough in his task in an effort to prove his own daughter right in her suspicions?

"Aye, send for the pricker," the king said after a long pause. "But delay until tomorrow. I want the prisoner denied food and sleep so he might be easier to contend with when the pricker begins his work. Escort the sorcerer back to his cell."

"Will no one hear me when I tell you I am innocent?" Lachlan's gaze traveled over the king, the Lord Advocate, Hugh Godfrey, the elders, and the crowd. "I am an innocent man."

The king averted his gaze. "Take him away before he casts a spell on us," he said above the growing cacophony of sound.

Lachlan struggled against the grip of the guards who came to seize him. The king would betray him in spite of their unique bond, regardless of how many enemies he had killed all in the king's name. He would toss Lachlan into the fires of hell simply to prove he alone could root out evil among his people.

The guards forced Lachlan forward. It took everything inside him to keep on walking despite the betrayal that racked his soul and knotted every muscle. The king had broken the sacred oath he and his brothers had taken when they'd become the king's Magnificent Seven.

Lachlan had been abandoned and left to the devices of others who would see that he was not only accused of witchcraft, but that he would suffer for that supposed crime as well. He was undone.

And yet, he had learned time and again in the heart of battle, that just when he thought all was lost, something would come along and remake him. Help him turn the tide. Help him win the day.

'Twas what he needed now. Someone or something to intervene—to cast a glimmer of light into the darkness. As though compelled by a force outside himself, he looked back over his shoulder and into Elizabeth's face.

Have faith, she mouthed the words to him. *I am with you.*

He continued to look at her until they dragged him through the doorway, cutting off his view. Even so, hope sprang to life within him. A bright burning flame that caught, flared, and grew. If Elizabeth stood by him in his most urgent hour of need, then there was hope he could yet survive whatever ordeal came at the end of John Swinton's needle.

CHAPTER TWELVE

THE GUARDS TOOK turns walking Lachlan back and forth across his small cell all through the night. The church had decreed that suspected witches and warlocks must be kept awake because during the hours of sleep, the Devil may easily enter their bodies and exert his power. The goal was to make the accused disoriented and confused so they might confess to their crimes more easily.

What the king or the church failed to consider was that as a warrior, Lachlan was used to long hours of wakefulness. One did not sleep when the enemy might attack. So, he plodded back and forth across the decaying, straw-strewn floor, enduring it all, for he knew this was not the worst of the challenges ahead of him.

When the tolbooth clock chimed eight times, the guards finally left him alone. Weary, but not beaten, he settled upon the cold stone floor, waiting. Lachlan did not have to wait long until footsteps sounded in the hallway. He heard the door of his cell creak open. The aureole of light cast by a torch illuminated the eager face of John Swinton. The similarity of his features to those of his daughter left no doubt about who he might be. He was dressed in a mud-colored monk's robe, complete with a rope belt tied about his ample belly. He shuffled into the chamber, giving Lachlan a better view of his soon-to-be torturer. His face was full, his lips hard, and his eyes studied Lachlan with cool objectivity. "Greetings of the day, m'laird. I am told you have been wicked among men and that it is up to me to uncover your sins."

"I have not said I am without sin," Lachlan clarified. "But what I am is no sorcerer. Your time with me shall be wasted, I fear."

"I very much doubt that. For I have yet to let a witch slip through my grasp." With a nod of his head, he instructed two guards to step forth and seize Lachlan. They escorted him out of the cell and down the long hallway until they came to a short staircase. The guards forced him down the stairs and into a stone chamber illuminated by a torch set into a sconce near the doorway. The only other light in the room came from a fire in the brazier at the far end of the chamber.

Eerie shadows crept over the contents of the room. But even in the low light, Lachlan could clearly make out a torture rack in the middle of the chamber.

"Help me." The weak and pitiful sound of a woman's voice jerked his attention to the left.

As his eyes adjusted to the low light, Lachlan saw that a young, blonde-haired woman sat upon a three-legged stool with her legs stretched before her and propped up by a slightly taller stool. Atop her legs were several iron bars that bit deep into her skin. Her back was flayed open from lashings as evidenced by the blood pooling on the floor beneath her. Listlessly, she turned her head toward Lachlan. His stomach pitched at the desperation in her eyes and the pain etched into every line of her weary face.

A moan sounded on his right. He turned toward the sound to see an older woman with gray hair, hanging from a hook in the ceiling with her arms tied behind her back. The woman's head lolled forward as though she had suddenly fainted. Weights were tied to her ankles, no doubt to increase her pain.

At the sight of the women suffering, Lachlan tensed. He twisted violently, sending his manacled hands into the belly of first one guard who held him, then the other. Both released their grip on him as they struggled to right themselves. Before Swinton could react, Lachlan advanced, wrapping the chain of his bonds around Swinton's neck and pulling him back against his own body.

The guards drew their swords, but stopped when Lachlan pulled the chains tighter until Swinton's face turned red. "Release these women, or I will kill him," Lachlan threatened.

Both guards looked to Swinton, who managed a small nod of his head. One guard removed the weight from the older woman's legs before lowering her down from the ceiling. He deposited her on the floor where she shivered uncontrollably, then vomited. The other guard removed the iron bars from the blonde-haired girl. As he did, she screamed in pain as the feeling returned to her legs. She tried to stand, but instead fainted, collapsing on the floor.

"What ... would you ... have me do ... with them now?" Swinton struggled to ask as the chains still cut into his flesh.

"I only want their suffering to end."

"You've only hastened ... their deaths ... and yours."

He had realized such the moment he acted, but he'd had to do something. "If you will not release them, then at least return them to their cells and give them something to eat and drink."

Swinton nodded as much as the chains at his throat would allow. Obeying orders, the guards helped the women to stand and half-carried, half-dragged them from the chamber.

Lachlan knew he would never make it out of the tolbooth alive if he tried to use Swinton as his prisoner or as a shield when the guards who had left sent for reinforcements. The only option available to him in such a secure place and on his own was to release the man and let him continue. He had no doubt his impending torture would be extreme because of his own actions.

Footsteps pounded down the stairs as Lachlan released Swinton. Six guards flooded the chamber and took Lachlan to the ground. The stone floor slammed against his back.

"Strip him down and get him on the rack," Swinton growled to the guards.

With little hope of fighting them off, Lachlan allowed the men to undress him. When they were done, they secured him to the rack at his feet and his waist. His manacled hands were brought up and tied over his head. He became chillingly aware of the cool, damp air that also carried the fetid odor of blood, urine, and death. Lachlan shivered.

Swinton smiled. "Not so brave now, are you?"

"I'll not give you the satisfaction you seek." Lachlan forced his features to harden and his body to tense. Swinton wanted his fear. He could see it in the man's beady eyes.

"We'll see about that." Swinton moved to a table along the far wall that bore a witch's bridle, thumb screws, a lead sprinkler, various weights and ropes, manacles of all sizes, a breast ripper, a cat-o-nine-tails, crocodile shears, and a head crusher.

The sight of the instruments of torture brought forth a shudder of revulsion. He'd heard about torture techniques over the years, but had never seen any of the devices used to accomplish that feat in person until now.

Swinton came to Lachlan's side and looked down at him with cool, unfeeling eyes. "Are you ready?" Swinton's hand drifted to a leather sheath attached to his belt from which he withdrew a long, cylindrical, brass needle that tapered to a fine point. "Where should we start?"

CHAPTER THIRTEEN

IT WAS CLOSE to midnight when the guards returned Lachlan to his cell. Elizabeth had waited there in the shadows since they'd taken him away hours ago. She'd paid one of the guards to bring fresh straw from the slaughterhouse, which after she'd swept the rotting straw into a corner, she'd spread out across the floor. And she'd traded her mother's pearl ring for fresh water and linen to be delivered upon Lachlan's return to his cell.

Reid and Lucy had left shortly after Lachlan and with the intent to head to the Nungate Inn at the edge of Berwick. They promised to send word to the other four of the king's elite guard, claiming that together they might hold some sway over the king.

Elizabeth could only hope they were right.

The tolbooth clock struck twelve when the guards dragged a naked Lachlan into the cell and tossed him on the floor face down. A pile of clothing was hurled next to him.

Elizabeth dropped to her knees beside him. She swayed, trying to fight back the tears and darkness that threatened to consume her. She had to be strong for Lachlan's sake.

"Where is my water and linen?" she called, drawing strength from the act of doing something to help him.

"Coming," a deep voice replied from the doorway.

Sweet Mary, he was barely breathing.

The young guard she had bribed entered and set down a basin of water, several lengths of white linen, and a candle that cast a soft yellow glow over the small cell. "Help me roll him over," Elizabeth demanded. When the guard did, she gasped at the sight of his welted and pierced flesh. Her stomach pitched.

"What did they do to him?" *Terrible things. Cruel and senseless things.* "I thought he was seeing the pricker?"

The guard nodded. "That was afore he decided tae rescue two other women who were bein' tortured there."

The tears she'd been trying to stop spilled past her lashes. "Thank you for these things," she said to the guard, "and for the time alone with my husband."

The guard looked down at the ring on his little finger. "My wife'll thank me fer this fer years tae come." He stood and exited the cell, locking the door behind him.

Looking at the man before her, Elizabeth felt utter despair. "We promised to keep each other from harm." She expelled a shattered breath. "At the first test of that promise, I failed. I'm so sorry. I'll figure a way out of this mess that my father has brought down on us both. I'll find a way." A swift jolt of agony shook Elizabeth.

Only a short time ago she had thought of this man as her

enemy. But over the past few days they had built a bridge that was spanning the gap between enemies and friends. She had actually been eager to see where things led after they had arrived at his castle . . . but would they even get a chance to move forward?

Heaviness settled in her chest as she dipped one of the pieces of linen into the water and began wiping the blood first from his forehead, then his cheeks and neck. She could feel a pulse beneath her fingertips that was thready, but strong.

She dipped her linen in the water, turning the liquid pink as she continued to gently clean his shoulders, his chest. When she reached the most male part of him, she cleaned him quickly before moving on to his legs.

He let out an occasional moan, but did not wake up, for which she was grateful.

When she was done cleansing the multitude of wounds, she secured linen around the worst ones in an effort to keep them from turning putrid, before she attempted to pull on his breeches and shirt in order to keep his wounds from further contamination due to the filthy conditions.

Elizabeth had to keep herself busy with his care so she couldn't think about the pain he must be feeling or how many deaths had occurred in this very place to those who were tortured like Lachlan had been.

She steeled herself to keep back the tears as she settled on the floor and cradled Lachlan's head in her lap. They needed a plan, and fast, before he was forced to endure anything more. Yet the harder she tried to assess the situation and make plans, the more jumbled her thoughts became.

With a sigh of capitulation, she leaned her head back against the cold, stone wall, appreciative of the fact they were both still alive. And until either she could see a clear path ahead, or the king's warriors could find a way out of this situation, neither of them would have any sort of future—separate or together.

"ELIZABETH."

The candle had long since sputtered itself out when Lachlan opened his eyes. He stared up at Elizabeth who drowsily opened her eyes.

"Elizabeth," he whispered again.

Instantly alert, she looked down at him. "You are awake."

"How did you get in here?"

Her brow furrowed. "It doesn't matter."

"It does to me." He shifted in her lap and pain fired through him. He gasped at the force of it even as he willed himself to relax.

"I bribed the guard." She reached down but refrained from stroking his cheek. "How do you feel?"

"Bruised. Pained." He lifted his head for a moment before settling it in her lap once more. "Weak." He frowned. "Have you been here all night?"

She nodded. "Lachlan—"

"This was not your fault," he interrupted.

"That is kind of you to say."

"It's the truth," he said as he struggled to a sitting position.

"What are you doing? Your wounds—"

"Hurt like hell," he said between clenched teeth.

"You were tortured to within an inch of your life less than six hours ago, and now you're behaving as if nothing happened! I thought you were dead when they brought you in here last night. There was so much blood . . ."

The sadness in her eyes made his throat tighten. "It takes more than that to kill a Douglas." He reached down and gently stroked a lock of hair away from her temple. "I'll never confess to the charges before me, no matter what they do. But I do need to think . . . to devise a plan . . ."

"I've been trying to think of a way out of this all night and I can think of nothing." Her words were barely above a whisper.

"Then I'll fight."

The sadness vanished and fire lit her eyes once more. "Fight what? Superstition? The king? Those are battles you cannot win." She stood and glared at him. "At least not alone."

"Nay." His frown deepened. "*You* aren't going to help

me with anything."

His thoughts moved back to the two women who'd been with him in the chamber of tortures. The younger of the two was around Elizabeth's age. "No one is safe from an accusation of witchcraft. You need to leave here, now, while you still can. I can endure whatever they do to me as long as I know you are safe."

Elizabeth planted her hands on her hips. "You saved my life not so many days ago," she said with an intensity that caused her voice to tremble. "It is my turn to save yours."

God's teeth, she was stubborn, Lachlan thought, trying to smother a spark of admiration tempering his feeling of annoyance. "Is this about our slates being wiped clean? A life for a life? Or is there more?"

Something flickered in her eyes a heartbeat before it vanished. "It's about saving your life. Once we get past that, we can look to other things."

Lachlan frowned, then flinched from the pain. He hadn't known her long enough to know every little expression that crossed her face, but if he had to guess he would say that brief flicker had been fear. Perhaps she was trying to save him to soothe her own soul, but deep inside she still believed he was all the things they said about him. The thought sent a chill down his spine. "Elizabeth—"

"Wait!" she said, her face suddenly alight in the semi-darkness. "It is not the tribunal we need to convince of your innocence. It is King James." She paced the confines of the small cell. "Would you say King James is a learned man? A logical man?"

Lachlan's frown deepened. "Aye. He is."

"Then we need to appeal to the logical side of him. Make him see through the preposterous charges my father and others have brought up against you."

"And how do you suppose we do that?" Lachlan asked.

"With counter evidence." She smiled. "I will dispel every charge, one by one by finding those who have given evidence against you and reversing their claims. Starting with myself."

"You did not testify against me."

"Not yet, but that moment will come and soon. Mark my words."

He stood and shuttered as pain rippled through him. "I don't understand."

"They say you tried to sacrifice me at Ravenscraig Castle. I intend to submit to an examination by someone who can confirm that I am still a maid."

"Nay, Elizabeth. I will not have you humble yourself in that way for me."

He saw the shimmer of tears in her eyes. "Do you wish to live?"

"Aye."

She stared at him, and the bleakness in her gaze was almost too much to bear. "I don't know what else to do. If it helps you to be freed from this place, then it will be worthwhile." She drew a deep breath as if to maintain her composure. "I do not want you to die, not in this way."

"Elizabeth," he said, and ignoring the pain, he took her into his arms. She tensed for a heartbeat before she relaxed. "I have no intention of dying."

"Finally, we agree on something." Despite her attempt at humor, her eyes still held fear as she touched his rough, unshaven jaw then pushed up on her toes and kissed him tenderly.

He gathered her closer, and much to his surprise, she deepened the kiss and molded her body to his. He blocked out the pain, focusing instead on the feel of her, the taste of her. The moment stretched before them. He seized it, used it to show her what she meant to him, in case he never got the chance to tell her anything more. He wanted her to know how much he needed her, wanted her, desired her. He reveled in the heat, allowing the warmth to heal his skin. He wanted so much more, but it was the wrong time, the wrong place.

Easing back from the kiss, he lifted his head and looked down into dazed brown eyes filled with desire. He knew a moment of intense satisfaction that he would hold dear in the minutes, hours, and days ahead to give him strength.

The sound of a throat clearing hauled his mind from his thoughts. Looking up, he saw the younger of his guards at the door neither of them had heard open.

"'Tis time fer ye tae leave, milady. The others will be arrivin' soon and I dinna want tae lose my job."

Elizabeth stepped back. Chill morning air filled the space between them and Lachlan shivered involuntarily. He wanted nothing more than to kiss her again, but he knew he had to let her go. "Whatever you decide to do, you must proceed carefully. Speak with Reid. He will know how to help. Promise you will."

She nodded. "I promise."

He watched her go. Watched the door close slowly behind her. As soon as the latch slid home, he sagged against the wall for support. While in Elizabeth's presence it had taken everything inside him to be strong, brave, unshaken.

He'd thought he'd known what fear was before—the shiver down his spine, the knot in his stomach, the metallic taste on his tongue. But those old experiences were nothing.

The fear inside him now was a living, breathing thing, which crept into every cell of his being like a macabre specter threatening to plunge him into eternal darkness.

He curled his hand at his sides, fighting the fear, willing it away. He dragged in a breath past the constriction in his chest. He was going to die, here and now, either in the torture chamber as John Swinton crushed his bones to gain a confession, or at the end of a noose. All that stood between him and death was Elizabeth.

Lachlan swallowed a lump in his throat. To survive the next few days he needed internal strength and faith and hope. He squeezed his eyes shut, battling the pain with everything inside him. *Be strong and courageous. Do not be afraid or terrified because of them, for the Lord your God goes with you; he will never leave you nor forsake you.* The thought came out of nowhere, reminding him that he wasn't alone, and that faith was his for the asking.

"Help me," he whispered, wishing God would hear his simple prayer, but not expecting him to. God never answered his prayers. Why would he start now?

CHAPTER FOURTEEN

C LOUDS FILLED THE morning sky so Elizabeth could not judge the hour as she hurried past the Old Parish church on her way to the Nungate Inn. She'd been told Laird and Lady Douglas had taken a room there. It was urgent she speak to them before Lachlan suffered any more.

The streets had been relatively quiet up until she turned a corner at the market cross and came upon a crowd. Their excited chattering grew louder the closer she got to whatever they were gathering around. She had to shift her steps left and then right, finding gaps in the throng to make any kind of progress forward.

At the next open space, she craned her neck to see what was happening. That's when she saw it—the gallows with a single long rope dangling down, waiting for its next victim.

The crowd parted then, giving Elizabeth a better view. At the base of the gallows stood two women—one older, and the other about the same age as herself. Both of their faces were nearly as pale as the white linen hoods covering their hair. They wore brown dresses made from coarse wool with a white collar and cuffs. The executioner on the platform walked slowly back and forth before the crowd, raising his arms, inciting them to cheer all the louder as another man below forced the older woman up a ladder, making her climb toward a platform above.

The first woman's legs were visibly trembling, no doubt with fear, as she tried to hoist herself up. Without warning, the man below pushed the old woman upward so violently she stumbled onto the platform. Unable to stop herself from falling, she slammed against the wood with a cry of pain.

Elizabeth stood motionless, and her breath caught as the crowd laughed and jeered in response. The poor woman had obviously been accused as a witch. From the bruises on her face and neck, she had clearly suffered some kind of torture as well, just as Lachlan had. And now that she'd been found guilty, she would be hanged.

The executioner on the platform jabbed at the old woman with his boot. "Get up, Witch!"

With considerable effort, the gray-haired woman finally gained her feet only to be jerked forward until she was forced up on to a stool and the noose was slipped over her head.

A row of dignitaries was seated on the right side of the platform, and the old woman's gaze shifted to them, searching their faces before moving on to the crowd. There was no malice in her expression, only surrender, and perhaps a touch of serenity at the realization that all her suffering would soon be at an end.

When the woman's gaze landed on Elizabeth, her heart

stumbled. Never in her life had she felt so powerless as in that moment. There was not a thing she could do to help the woman without great cost to herself. Elizabeth returned her gaze, hoping the woman could read the sympathy she felt.

A glimmer of a smile came to the old woman's lips before she bowed her head, staring at her feet.

One of the dignitaries rose and held up his hand, seeking silence. "Good people," he shouted. "We are here today to witness the just punishment of this woman who made a pact with the Devil to carry out his evil designs here on earth." He gestured toward the old woman.

"Ye witches! Ye loathsome creatures!"

"Burn the witches! Burn them in hell-fire!"

The man held up his hand to silence the cries erupting from the crowd. When they fell silent, he read the charges against her. "Agnes Quarie, these are the charges of which you have been declared guilty. You are guilty of consulting with a known witch. Guilty of abusing the people and cursing the same, especially Grissel Thomson's bairn that he was born with a clubbed foot. Guilty of laying a curse on Ellie Knox's hens that they laid no more. Guilty of possession by the Devil." He turned to Agnes. "Do ye have any last words, Agnes Quarie?"

She lifted her head and spoke, but her words were drowned out by cheers from the crowd. Before she could finish, the stool was kicked out from beneath her.

"She's dancin' to the Devil's song now!" As her feet

kicked and jerked, the crowd jeered and whistled their approval. Finally, her slight body went limp and her tongue protruded from her mouth. Slowly, her slack body turned in a half circle in the soft breeze, then twisted back again.

With tears in her eyes, Elizabeth watched as two town guards on the platform stepped forward to take Agnes down. After she was examined by the doctor and declared dead, the guards carried her remains to the pyre to be burned.

Before Agnes was tossed into the flames, the next to be hanged was forced up the ladder and onto the platform. The blonde-haired woman's beautiful face was filled with fear as she stepped onto the stool Agnes's feet had last mounted.

Once again, the charges were read by the dignitary. "Isobel Craig, you are guilty of bewitching three men with charms and witchcraft."

The charges were harsh and ugly as they were carried away by the morning air. The poor girl on the platform would be hanged simply because she was pretty and had spurned the advances of three men. Elizabeth's throat tightened and her tears fell all the harder now. Where was the justice in all of this? Agnes and Isobel could have been just as innocent of the charges against them as Lachlan was, yet no one seemed to care.

Before the stool was kicked from beneath her, Isobel's lips moved slightly as though she was saying a prayer, which ended swiftly as the stool tilted. As her body was removed from the noose, a magpie flew from a copse of bushes nearby and settled on the crosspiece of the gallows. It uttered a dry, throaty rattle three times before it flew off again.

"See!" A man in the front of the crowd shouted. "The Devil comes for his own."

The crowd responded with jeers as the two guards tossed Isobel's body into the flames. Elizabeth shifted away, not wanting to watch as a great pall of smoke filled the air. But because of the dense crowd, her progress forward was slowed and she couldn't help but notice the flames of the pyre leapt higher and higher as the women's hair caught fire and their skin blackened. The stench of burning flesh overpowered all else and it was all Elizabeth could do to keep from retching.

Drawing shallow breaths, she focused her sight on the distance, even as her stomach twisted at the hissing sound, like rashers frying on a griddle, which followed her as she struggled to leave the gallows behind. By nightfall, all that would be left of the two women would be a pile of ash.

Elizabeth shoved her way through the crowd now. She had to get away from the reminder of what might yet happen to Lachlan if she couldn't find a way to set him free. Relief filled her at the sight of the Nungate Inn ahead. She was breathless from running when she finally threw open the door and burst into the common room.

Several gazes turned her way when she entered—some of those gazes filled with fear, others with disgust before they turned away. At the patrons' responses, Elizabeth looked down at her clothing to see they were not only dusty from her race through the village, but also streaked with blood from her time in the cell with Lachlan.

She lifted her chin, ignoring her disheveled state. She glanced around the crowded chamber in the low light, searching for Reid and Lucy. She spotted them in a corner with three other men, one whom she recognized as Cameron Sinclair. She hurried over. "I must speak with you, Laird Douglas."

Reid's chair scraped back as he stood to face her. His features filled with surprise then horror.

"Good heavens," Lucy gasped beside her husband. "What has happened to you?"

"I bribed the guard at the tolbooth to let me in to see Lachlan. I waited for hours until they finally brought him." Her voice caught. "If he stays there much longer, they'll kill him from the torture alone."

Reid stood and took her hands in his. "Come, join us, Elizabeth." Reid offered her his chair. He pulled another over from the table next to them and sat. "I'd like to introduce you to the men who can help Lachlan."

KING JAMES FROWNED as he looked about the sparsely furnished chamber where his men had bade him to meet them this morning. Could they not have chosen a more elegant setting? Something worthy of a king? But then again, this was a clandestine meeting. No doubt to make an appeal for him to release their accused brother-in-arms. His gaze moved to the men gathered around the small table: Reid and Quinn Douglas, Cameron Sinclair, Malcolm Hamilton, Rhys Elliot, and Alexander Ross. The only one of the seven who was missing was currently in gaol, charged as a warlock.

"Be quick about it." James scowled at the remaining six of his Magnificent Seven. "Why have you interrupted my day for such a meeting?"

Reid Douglas stood, then offered a stiff bow. "I respect that Your Grace is a very busy man, therefore I will not ramble on and on about the reasons you should release my cousin, Lachlan. Instead I will simply put forth that as your humble servant, the seeker of your justice, and the keeper of the kingdom, that you should drop all charges against Lachlan Douglas and place him into our care. A failure to do so could jeopardize your relationship with all those gathered here."

Fury flashed through King James, so hard and fast, he felt dizzy with it. He thumped his fist on the table. "You dare to challenge my authority?"

Reid Douglas never broke eye contact, but the wrinkles around his eyes seemed to deepen. "In this matter, aye, for we know Lachlan to be innocent of all charges against him. And if you are honest with yourself, so do you. Donald Ruthven and his clan fabricated every situation for their own benefit in order to retaliate against both you and the Douglases."

At his words, King James lost his hold on his anger. Why had he ever agreed to his wife's suggestion that he betroth Lachlan Douglas to Elizabeth Ruthven? Any attempt at peace had obviously gone far astray.

Reid continued to stare him down.

"What would you have me do? God, Himself, urged my mother to pass the Witchcraft Act into law. There is no punishment too severe for any man or woman who is found guilty of practicing or abetting witchcraft in all its forms, sorcery, necromancy, fortune-telling, or healing. All these are punishable by death. I cannot defy my God."

Beside Reid, his twin brother's brows pulled together slowly. "It is not God's will that innocent people be tortured and murdered. It is yours," Quinn Douglas said.

James's anger spiked once more. "Mind yourself, Douglas."

"Your Grace, we are not asking you to empty your gaols," Reid said with a look of reprimand at his brother. "Just as we all fight for you, in search of justice, we ask that you look a little deeper into these charges against Lachlan. Do not accept them at face value. Ruthven followed Lachlan and Elizabeth from the moment they left Falkland Palace, seeking to engage in battle in order to stop Elizabeth from becoming a Douglas. That he chose not a battle of swords, but a battle of misdeeds and misdirection should be enough to give you pause."

"I will not suffer obstinacy, Laird Douglas." The king frowned at each man seated around the table. "Not from any of you. If you defy me, you might find yourselves in a cell alongside your brother-in-arms."

"Lachlan is falsely accused," Alexander Ross said. "To a man, we will swear on a Bible to attest to his innocence."

"That is all well and good, but the charges still stand. Lachlan is accused of sorcery. It matters not that Ruthven is the instigator of it all," the king replied.

"It matters to us." Cameron Sinclair stood and, with fury in his eyes, he drew his sword, setting it on the table in front of King James. "And, since you refuse to see reason, I will be the first to break my vow of allegiance to you."

Rhys Elliot followed Cameron to his feet, setting his sword beside his brother's. "If we all breach our vow of protecting you, how well would you fare among the den of vipers who reside in your court?"

"Without us at your side, you will not be safe." Malcolm Hamilton stood and set his sword beside Cameron's.

Then both of the Douglas twins stood, followed by Alexander Ross, until all their swords lay before the king. "We stand together or not at all."

The reality of their actions hit James like a blow to the chest. He struggled to his feet, staring them down. "I could strip you of your rank. I could seize your assets." Spittle formed at the edges of his mouth.

"Of course, you could," Reid Douglas agreed. "And you

could be skewered by a dagger on the street outside this meeting place if you leave here without protection."

King James gaped at the man. He'd never felt such a confusing jumble of rage and fear. His head was spinning with the thoughts, possibilities, fears of what might happen to him without his personal guards. "I could banish you from this country."

"Aye," Reid continued, "and the moment we are gone, your enemies will converge, hiding in every shadow. You won't be able to eat, drink, walk, or sleep without fearing who you can truly trust." He shrugged. "The choice is yours, after all . . . you are the king."

The truth crept over King James. He realized the significance of what Reid Douglas said. There had already been several attempts on his life. He'd been kidnapped and held prisoner as well by none other than the Ruthvens. He looked about the room at the men gathered before him. He had chosen all of these men for a reason at one time—they were unequalled in strength, courage, and spirit. It was those same qualities they portrayed to him right now all for the sake of protecting one of their own.

They stared long and hard at each other, and James knew neither he nor any of them were used to losing a battle. Finally, he said, "How about a compromise?"

The men looked at each other and then sat down. "We're listening," Reid said.

"I cannot withdraw the charges that have already been

recorded in the court documents. However, I can move Lachlan from Haddington tolbooth and place him in a private chamber in a nearby inn under constant guard until his trial."

"And you can see he endures no more torture," Quinn Douglas added.

King James gave a quick nod. "'Tis the least I can do for one of my own."

"And the charges against him, how do we dismiss those?" Cameron Sinclair asked.

"If Reid and Quinn will stay here to protect me, I will give the rest of you the freedom to track down those who gave testimony and bring them here for questioning by no one but myself. By the powers given me by God himself, I will know if someone is lying."

"Consider it done," Reid said with a nod to Quinn. "You know you can trust us to keep you safe."

"Then take back your swords so you can accomplish that feat," he growled as he stood.

His men stood and collected their weapons. As they did, he looked at each one. "Consider this the one and only time I will allow you all to persuade me from my purpose in this life. My word is law. Remember that from this moment forward."

Reid bowed. "We are fortunate to have such a wise and generous king."

"Indeed, you are," King James replied as he headed for

the door with two of his guardsmen at his side.

After the king had left, it was decided that Malcolm Hamilton would head to the Buckhaven Inn and return with Bessie Broun, her husband, as well as Jane and Meg Wenham. Rhys Elliot would depart for Edinburgh to find Roland Carswell and force the young minister to appear before the court. Cameron Sinclair would head back to Ravenscraig Castle to collect both Mariam Swinton and any of the fishermen he could find before returning to Haddington. And Alexander Ross would travel with Sinclair as far as Aberlady where he would search for the remaining fishermen, a mysterious black cat, and also bring the innkeeper of the Cairn Inn back to the court to testify.

With luck, they would accomplish these deeds before Lachlan was to appear before the tribunal again.

CHAPTER FIFTEEN

LACHLAN WAS IN the midst of a dream where he was waiting at the gates of Whittingehame for Elizabeth to come home to him. The morning mists faded as the sky overhead brightened. And he heard her calling his name. "Douglas." And louder a second time.

Suddenly Lachlan was yanked back to reality, startled awake, to find a man bending over him, his rancid breath in Lachlan's face.

"Wake up, sorcerer, before I toss ye with cold water!" the man taunted as his fingers gripped tight around Lachlan's arm. "Time to get up."

For a moment, Lachlan wasn't certain where he was. The dream had left him disoriented. But then he felt the weight of the manacles on his hands, the cold stone beneath him, and the straw that scratched his cheek, and it all rushed back.

He was in gaol. He'd been tortured. Was the man here to take him to Swinton again? After Elizabeth had left, Swinton had come back, and instead of taking him to the torture chamber, he had striped him there, in his cell, and he'd endured twenty more lashes.

One . . . two . . . three lashes had fallen on his back. Despite his determination to remain unaffected by the lash, a gasp escaped his throat as a sharp stab of intense pain tore through his already abused back.

The slip of sound had made Swinton smile. "Ready for three more?"

"Why don't you just kill me now?" Lachlan struggled to keep the fear from his voice. He had to stay in control. He didn't fear dying, but the pain was wearing him down. "I'll never admit to the charges against me."

Swinton's smile slipped and became a frown. "Every moment of every day will be filled with slow agony until I get what I want."

Three more lashes struck his back, leaving red welts burning against his flesh. Lachlan clenched his jaw.

Swinton might be ruthless, but he was no match for Lachlan's own resolve. No amount of torture could pry a confession from him. And no force under Heaven would ever make him reveal the names of others who might be witches just to make his torment stop.

"Perhaps you need more persuasion," Swinton growled as he gave him six more lashes, then six more, and more, until Lachlan trembled from the pain. Had that memory been days ago, hours, or only minutes? He no longer knew, except that it seemed like forever.

But now a different man stood over him. "What are you waiting for?" the man asked as his eyes glittered with a strange illumination cast upon his face by the torch. "The king has requested you be moved to better quarters, and that his physician attend you."

Overwhelmed with emotion at the thought of no more torture, Lachlan sucked in a relieved breath. "I am freed?"

"Nay," the man said, helping Lachlan stand. "'Tis simply a reprieve. But if I were ye, I'd be grateful fer that much. Others here are nae so lucky as that tae have friends in high places."

King James, a friend? More like a madman. But Lachlan wasn't about to argue if it meant putting some distance between himself and this place. He staggered to his feet and gratefully followed the man from his cell and into the bright light of day.

Outside the tolbooth, Lachlan recoiled from the light. After days of darkness, the sunlit sky was almost too much. He squeezed his eyes shut.

"Hurry up," the man who'd released him said with a tug on Lachlan's manacled hands.

"Give me a moment." Lachlan remained where he stood, breathing in the fresh air, letting it slide through his lungs before exhaling. After a few moments, he slowly opened his eyes, allowing them to adjust to the bright light before he started forward once more.

A carriage waited several steps away. "Get in. Ye're tae be delivered tae Haddington Tower. They've made up a room fer ye there. I'll be yer warder. So, if ye make things easy fer me, I'll make things easy fer ye. Agreed?"

Lachlan could only nod his agreement as it took all his energy to climb into the carriage and collapse back against the squabs. Pain sizzled along his nerves, his flesh, his back but he barely let the sensations register. All he could think about was perhaps, heaven help him, perhaps there was hope to survive.

ELIZABETH STEPPED PAST the guard and into the room the king had made for her husband at the top of Haddington Tower. At the sight of Lachlan curled on his side on a narrow bed her heart stumbled. His clothing was soaked in blood and manacles still bound his hands. She turned back to the guard. "Please take him out of his chains."

"I cannot."

"Where can he go?" she pleaded, with her heart in her throat. "Can you not see he is in no condition to fight you or anyone?"

The guard pressed his lips together as his gaze shifted from Elizabeth to his prisoner then back again. "As you wish," he finally agreed.

With one of the keys attached to a ring on his belt, the guard unlocked the manacles. They clanked against the floor. At the sound, Lachlan's eyes opened and his hands flexed as though testing the feel of freedom once more.

The guard turned toward the door, but Elizabeth stayed him with a hand on his arm. "Might I ask one more favor? I will see you are compensated handsomely if you will find me a basin of water, and send someone to the Nungate Inn and ask Reid Douglas to send his cousin a spare set of clothes."

"I'll see what I can do," the guard said, then left.

She had brought salve, fresh linens, and a tincture for pain that Quinn's wife, Vivian, had sent to Haddington with her husband. As a healer who had suffered herself under King James's quest to rid all Scotland of evil, Vivian would know what to send to help Lachlan heal from his wounds.

Elizabeth moved to the bed and sank to her knees beside Lachlan. "My God, what have they done to you?"

Pain reflected in the depths of Lachlan's blue eyes. "Nothing that I will not survive." Bright red splashes of blood seeped through the back of his muslin shirt.

Trying to be brave for him, Elizabeth forced her own emotions aside as she helped him into a sitting position. He winced with pain and his breathing was ragged, as she propped him up with pillows against his back and with his head resting on the headboard of the bed. She opened the satchel she carried, removing the contents and laying them next to the bed: a pile of fresh linen, a jar of salve, a bottle of tincture, a needle and thread, as well as a large portion of salted meat, bread, and cheese. "Vivian created a tincture to help with the pain," she said as she opened the bottle then held it to his lips, tipping it up and allowing the liquid to run into his throat.

When she had given him a dose, she sank back on her knees and waited. After only a few labored breaths, his shoulders relaxed and he settled into the pillows more deeply. Elizabeth breathed a thankful sigh.

"I'm so glad to see you—" He stopped abruptly as the door opened. The guard entered, carrying a basin of steaming water, which he set by Elizabeth's side.

"Thank you," she said.

He nodded. "I sent a man to the inn. He should be back soon with the clothing you asked for."

Again, she offered her thanks before the guard left. When he was gone, she rose up on her knees once more and took Lachlan's hand in hers. He squeezed her fingers so gently at first that it took a moment to realize that he'd done it. He was so weak. "Vivian also sent a healing salve. But first I must wash your wounds."

"Do what you must."

Elizabeth stood, then bent to remove his shirt, easing him slightly away from the pillows to pull it up and over his head. At the sight of his back, she gasped. A multitude of red welts crisscrossed his flesh—two of the stripes were open and bleeding. "I will need to sew a few of these wounds together if they are to heal properly."

"A warrior's life is harsh." Lachlan's voice brought her gaze to his face. He assessed her. For what? Revulsion? Fear?

She straightened her shoulders. He would see no weakness in her. "You need not apologize. We all have scars, Lachlan. Some of us wear them on the outside, others on the inside."

"And your scars? Are they inside or out?"

"We aren't discussing my scars. Yours are the only ones of interest at this moment."

Lachlan's eyes pinned her in place. She had a sudden terrifying feeling that he could see inside her, see the very scars she talked about—those left by the death of her mother. She swallowed hard then lifted her chin. "Elizabeth," he said softly. "It's not weakness to be afraid, or to be vulnerable in front of others." His words were slightly slurred as the effects of the tincture set in.

"I'm not afraid," she assured him, but she did fear being vulnerable. She pushed the thought away, forcing herself to focus on the task at hand. "Come, let's turn you onto your stomach. The worst of the wounds are on your back. I need to tend those first." He settled his head on the pillow, facing her. As he relaxed, Elizabeth picked up the needle. She ran the metal through a hot flame before she threaded it and set to work, sewing the edges of the first wound closed.

The room suddenly seemed too warm, the air too thick, as she started work on the second open wound. She bent so close to him, she could perceive the tightening of his muscles, the increased rhythm of his breathing. Her stitches were even and steady as she tied the thread off. Silence stretched between them, broken only by the gentle duet of their breathing.

She glanced at his face, and her breath caught. In that moment she saw past the blood and grime still covering his face to the true handsomeness there. Golden hair framed his face, a face that held not brutality and menace, but determination and kindness.

It was the kind of face a woman couldn't help but stare at in awe and with desire. With gentleness, she brushed a lock of hair from his eyes. Her hand strayed to the strong, straight line of his cheekbone, and down to his chin. "I'm so sorry to bring you pain," she whispered.

A faint smile came to his lips and a curious light filled his eyes. "I hardly felt a thing."

Elizabeth curled her fingers against the light flutter that took flight in her stomach, before she returned to her sewing. When she was done, she thoroughly cleansed his back, and applied the salve before winding fresh linen over his wounds, and praying they would heal well.

When she was done, she turned him over. "Are the pillows soft enough? I can try to find something softer."

He grimaced as he leaned back into the pillows. "These are an absolute blessing compared to what I had before."

Elizabeth noted the lines of tension around Lachlan's mouth and eyes. When had she become so familiar with the expressions on his face? Needing a distraction, she spread salve on the prick marks over his chest and arms.

"Elizabeth." When she wouldn't meet his gaze, he

stopped her hand from spreading more salve. "You are not responsible for my injuries or my pain."

"So much has happened since our wedding," she admitted, meeting his gaze.

"Aye." He laced his fingers through hers, his grip strong and excruciatingly intimate. Then he tensed and pulled his hand from hers, staring down at her right hand. "Where is your mother's ring?"

"I traded it for entrance into your cell, and for fresh straw, clean water, and linens to help you heal."

He frowned. "You should not have done that."

"I had to."

Silence fell between them again until she said, "Your brothers-in-arms were all here. Reid and Quinn remain, but the others have dispersed to gather everyone who has given testimony against you. Within a day or two, all the evidence we need to free you will be here in Haddington. My father will no longer be able to maintain his falsehoods about what happened, and you will be set free." Tears came to her eyes. "Soon we will take back control of the situation. My father will not get the best of either of us."

"Thank you for all you did to make that happen." His touch softened as he leisurely stroked his thumb back and forth across the sensitive flesh of her palm. Her pulse accelerated.

"I didn't do much. Reid and Quinn had the same idea as I did about finding some way to disprove my father's lies.

Your brothers-in-arms are the ones who deserve the credit for heading in four different directions to gather everything quickly." She could not look away as her heart beat faster and the blood quickened in her veins.

"Have you seen your father since my arrest?"

She shook her head. "He was angry after I refused to return home with him. But I will need to confront him sooner or later."

"Make sure Reid or Quinn are with you when you do." He leaned closer until his lips were mere inches from hers.

She could see the pulse drumming in his temple. The warmth of his breath caressed her throat, causing her to tremble. He'd said it to her when they'd first married, that there would be a time when she would ask him, beg him to touch her, to kiss her, to make love to her.

Those thoughts filled her mind now as she brought her lips to his and the fire that had been smoldering between them for days leapt to life, and she wanted more. To her immense relief, so did he. He made no secret of his desire as his hands moved to her shoulders, then her back, hauling her deeper into his arms. He pressed against her and invited her in. There was nothing to prevent them from indulging the passion that flared so hotly, so powerfully, between them.

She felt the beating of his heart against her chest, echoing her own as he took charge of the kiss in that moment. He kissed her with unleashed passion, his tongue tangling with hers, then plunging and slowly retreating in some wildly exciting, forbidden rhythm that made the blood roar in her ears.

Her hand came up to rest against his chest, before she jerked it back, longing to touch him, but knowing she should not, not until he was more fully healed. She wanted to explore the man in her arms, to quench the tension that curled tauter, tighter in her belly . . . That moment would come after she'd had an examination by the king's physician on the morrow.

At the remembrance, she broke the kiss suddenly.

"Not yet," he whispered against her lips.

"We must stop," she said on a tortured breath. "I have an examination by the king's physician tomorrow to prove you did not harm me at Ravenscraig Castle. If you kiss me again, I'm not certain I will have the will to resist you."

His smile held sadness as well as sweetness. "You do not have to put yourself through all that for me. I know it was important for you to convince others our marriage was consummated when it was not. What's changed?"

She didn't look at him. "I've changed. You've changed. Our situation has changed."

With a finger beneath her chin, he brought her gaze back to his. "Change is an inevitable part of life. If you are not changing, then you are not living fully."

"There has been too much change for you lately. I need to see the physician because I need to believe there is some justice in this world or nothing makes sense." She glanced down at his bandaged chest. "If you, or I, suffer like this again, it will be because we believe what we are suffering for is worth the cost of the pain, not because of something my father orchestrated."

"Agreed," he said with a smile in his voice. He shifted his body to the side of the bed, and patted the now empty space beside him. "Come, sit by me, let me hold you in my arms."

"But your injuries—"

"Are feeling much better thanks to that tincture and your intoxicating kisses."

She moved beside him. He put his arm around her and pulled her closer until she laid her cheek against his shoulder. "Do you want to talk about what that man did to you? Will that help ease your suffering, to share it with me?"

"Nay!" His voice was harsh, strained. "I would never wish for you to know the horrors one human can inflict upon another. My memories will fade in time, especially with you at my side. Let us talk of something else."

Elizabeth felt an irrational rush of relief. She would have listened if he needed to talk, but the hideous memory of the hangings still lingered in her own mind. It was not her suffering, but a reminder as he'd said of what one person could legally do to another in these troublesome times. "You are one of the king's own men. Do you like being a soldier?" she asked, hoping to send the conversation in a different direction.

He shrugged. "I knew nothing else from the time I was a boy and sent to live with my cousins. My uncle and cousins seemed pleased with my skills."

"So, you took up the sword for the king?"

He made a face. "In these trying times, it seemed an appropriate profession. All of the seven grew rich from our efforts, not necessarily from the king's coffers, but from defeating our enemies and benefiting from the spoils of war."

"Did you like it?" she asked again.

"Nay. I've always found peace far more appealing than war."

"You are a landowner now, with fertile fields that stretch as far as the eye can see."

He gave her a lopsided smile. "Except that I am no farmer. I will leave the tending of the earth to the crofters. My interests lie elsewhere."

"Do they lean more toward the sea?" she asked, remembering how fondly he talked about discovering new lands and traveling to places yet unknown while they had been aboard *The Golden Rose.*

"Even before my arrest, I was growing tired of doing battle for the king's glory one day, then having him denounce our efforts the next." He leaned back against the pillows, gazing up at the ceiling. "One day I was on the docks in Aberdeen after a particularly difficult battle, watching a ship from Madagascar sail into port. The wind lifted the sails, and I could smell the scent of the sea and the cargo of cinnamon being unloaded and I suddenly knew I wanted to be a part of it—to sail away from Scotland and my past memories here. To explore new places—" He broke off and dropped his gaze to her face. "Is that something you could ever endure or possibly even enjoy?"

She returned his gaze, feeling an unfamiliar stirring in her chest. When they had first been forced together, she only knew about the raw brutality of his life and how it had forged him into the man he now was. But in the last few days, he'd shown her a gentler side that made him less of a powerful enigma and far more human. She understood him better, and with that understanding she was drawn to not only him, but also a life he could offer her that was different from anything she'd ever imagined. "I could enjoy such an adventure if it is at your side."

She expected to see pleasure in his eyes; instead his expression turned grim. "Then if we are to have any kind of future at all together, we must fight these charges of witchcraft."

"You didn't let what my clan did to you rob you of your dreams, don't let what Swinton did to you rob you of your joy. You don't want to give him such a victory."

He gazed at her a moment, then some of the passion he had shared a moment before returned to his eyes. "You are right. I won't let any of them take more from me than they already have. Dreams should be taken care of in a world where so few are realized."

She smiled up at him. "Tell me, Husband, what other dreams do you have?" It was better to focus on the future and not the difficulty of proving his innocence at the trial, which still lay ahead.

CHAPTER SIXTEEN

"THANK YOU FOR being here with me, Lucy," Elizabeth said as the two women waited for the king's physician in one of the bedchambers at Hardgate Manor where the king had taken residence for Lachlan's impending trial. Lucy had been kind enough to come with her once Elizabeth explained the situation.

"If not from you," Lucy asked with a frown, "then from where did all that blood come?"

Heat rushed into Elizabeth's cheeks. "'Twas my fault it was in the bed in the first place. I begged Lachlan to cover for the fact that we had not yet . . . that we . . ."

"I understand," Lucy said with a gentle touch on Elizabeth's arm.

"Lachlan went to the slaughterhouse and brought back blood that had been set aside from the stag we'd had for a banquet in our honor at Ravenscraig Castle." Elizabeth tensed, expecting to see pity when she brought her gaze back to Lucy's face. Instead, she was gifted with a look of understanding. "I was so filled with doubts and confusion about him then."

"And now?"

Elizabeth hesitated. Only one doubt remained, one that might have been fabricated by her father as all the witchcraft accusations against her husband had been. "I'll never really know him fully, just as he will not know me. Each day we are new persons based on the previous day's events and emotions."

Just then, a knock sounded on the door. "Enter," Elizabeth bade as a young page opened the door. He bowed low before he announced, "King James of Scotland."

The king swept past the young man, followed by an older gentleman whom Elizabeth assumed was the physician. King James's imposing figure filled the room at once. He was dressed in a dark blue doublet, slashed with red-gold silk.

Elizabeth and Lucy both rose to their feet and curtsied. "Your Grace, we are deeply honored by your attendance to his matter." The king came forward and offered Elizabeth his ringed hand. She dutifully kissed it briefly then stood.

"Let's get on with the examination," he demanded without further ceremony. He moved to a table near the hearth and poured himself a glass of wine before taking a seat and staring into the fire, ignoring them.

Elizabeth moved to the bed. She had already removed her slippers, garters, and hose. All the physician had to do was to flip up her skirts to examine her fully.

"Good morrow, Lady March. I will be conducting your examination," said a tall, thin man dressed in a pale yellow tunic. He advanced toward the bed with a cheerful smile. "I'm Dr. Parkins." He stopped at the bedside and took her hand, tapping it gently. "No need to fear, my dear. I'll make this as quick and as painless as possible. When you are ready, lie back."

On the other side of her, Lucy placed a hand on her shoulder and squeezed it affectionately.

Elizabeth glanced at the king, who still stared into the fire. For the gift of privacy, she was grateful. Ready to get the examination over with, she took a deep breath and held it as Dr. Parkins lifted her skirts over her knees. When he spread her legs apart and thrust two fingers inside of her, she gasped. Then just as quickly as he had entered her, he retreated.

"Very good," the doctor said cheerfully, as he lowered her skirts once more before turning to the king. "She is indeed intact, Your Grace. The blood on the sheets could not have been as a result of breaking her hymen. She is a virgin still. I shall write up my findings and enter them in the court records."

The king grunted and downed the contents of his glass before standing. The king swung to look at Elizabeth. A droplet of red liquid dribbled down his chin, but he did not seem to notice. "Of the five charges against your husband, this exam seems to prove him not guilty of one." His gaze narrowed. "There are still four others against him, so do not allow yourself to find any kind of hope in this revelation."

Elizabeth swung her legs over the bed and stood, staring resolutely ahead as she suspected the king was not through with her yet.

"I had trusted both you and Lachlan to take my offer of a truce between your two families seriously, like sensible, faithful subjects who obey their sovereign in all things." The color in the king's cheeks rose to match the drop of ruby liquid on the flesh above his beard.

"We needed time to adjust to each other, Your Grace. Time to put our feelings of hatred aside."

His gaze narrowed further. "You have both brought disgrace upon your families, and if you do not consummate this marriage between you tonight, then I will see that the other four charges against Lachlan hold, no matter what witnesses come forward and give testimony. And you," he said, as a vein at his temple began to throb noticeably, "I will see you given in marriage to a man of little means and in a desolate location far from all whom you might know and love. Do I make myself quite clear?"

Elizabeth's heart pounded in her chest as she nodded.

Then, as abruptly as he had come, he turned and left the room. When he was gone, and the physician with him, Elizabeth collapsed back upon the bed and clutched her trembling hands in her lap. "That man is utterly terrifying!"

Lucy laughed as she came around to Elizabeth's side of the bed and dropped down beside her. "At this moment I would have to agree, but I have seen a very different side of our king at another time in the not too distant past. One where he stood, trembling with fear in front of all his subjects."

Elizabeth gaped at her cousin by marriage. "Do tell, please, so that I might have something else to think about every time I am in his presence."

With a conspiratorial smile, Lucy told her about the time she had pretended to assassinate the king with her bow and arrow in his own court at Falkland Palace.

Bolstered by Lucy's story, Elizabeth quickly dressed and the two women left the Hardgate Manor, returning to the carriage that had brought them there. The carriage jerked forward as the horses were set in motion, forcing the two women back into the squabs.

"What will you do now?" Lucy asked as they headed back to Haddington.

"As I am ordered," Elizabeth said with a shy smile. "I wish to see my husband."

"Is he faring better now that he is at least out of a cell and away from Swinton?"

Elizabeth nodded, but could not stop a shudder that came at the memory of the striping to Lachlan's back. "He is healing and gaining strength. But how does one ever put that kind of abuse behind them?"

Lucy's lips turned up into a smile. "With your help and a little time and attention, I am certain he will be renewed."

"We still have the trial ahead—"

A horse neighed in agony. The carriage lurched and shuddered to a halt, throwing both Lucy and Elizabeth to their knees.

Lucy slowly rose and carefully peered out the window. The blade of a dagger pierced the wood beside her head, pointing into the frame. Lucy jerked back from the window, but not before retrieving the blade. She held it out to Elizabeth. "Take this. You might need it."

Crouched on the floor, she heard the shouts of men and the clashing of metal against metal mixing with the screams of the horses. "What is happening?" Elizabeth asked as she accepted the weapon.

Lucy reached into the folds of her skirt and pulled free a dagger she obviously kept hidden there. "There are several men attacking the carriage." Her expression deadly serious, she added, "One of them is your father."

"I refused to go with him after Lachlan was charged, and now he seeks to kidnap me instead." Elizabeth staunched the surge of emotion that threatened. "We must get out of here. I cannot let him take me. If he does, I may never see any of you again."

"Your own father would harm you?"

"Either harm me or hide me away where no one will ever find me. Then he'll blame my disappearance on the Douglases, and continue the feud for the next generation." Elizabeth raised herself up and peered through the window on the left side of the carriage. As she suspected from the sounds, all the fighting was coming from the right side. She cautiously opened the door and peered out. A copse of rowan trees was only a few yards away, and no one else was in sight. "Come. We can take cover in the trees."

Clutching the dagger in her hand, Elizabeth drew a deep breath and leapt from the carriage. With Lucy at her heels, she darted across the grassy road and into the gorse that lined the roadway before reaching the cover of the trees. Branches lashed at her face and arms as she pushed through the barrier.

"Stop!"

A sudden chill gripped her as she glanced over her shoulder to see not only her father, but also Keddy crashing through the gorse behind them.

Elizabeth ran faster, trying desperately to outdistance her father. Lucy kept pace beside her as they scrambled over the mossy forest floor that was riddled with exposed roots, rocks, and fallen logs. There was a stream on their left and another on their right, but they picked their way around the obstacles, keeping several paces ahead of their attackers.

Elizabeth's breath was coming in little gasps as they broke through the tree line and emerged into the open. Instantly the whoosh of wings filled the air as the birds resting there took flight. Once that sound dissipated, another took its place, that of the roar of a waterfall. They had come to the edge of a cliff.

Elizabeth and Lucy stopped, then turned back to the forest, their harsh breathing mingling with the rush of the water behind them. They couldn't go forward, and they could not go back toward her father and Keddy, who had stopped a few yards from them.

"There's no way out of this, Daughter, except leaping to your death," her father said between breaths.

Elizabeth swallowed hard. She had considered that once, and fortunately Lachlan had come along to stop her. "Nay, I have too much to live for, too many things that remain yet undone."

"Such as consummating your marriage?" Her father sneered. "I was outside the door at Hardgate Manor. I heard the king's demands. But I have my own demands. What you failed to accomplish shall never come to be between the Douglases and the Ruthvens. I would rather you die at my hand than let that vile man have you. Now put down your daggers, both of you, and come here."

Keddy and her father both held swords in their hands. The longer and stronger weapons would overwhelm two small daggers. She and Lucy might get in a few strikes if they attempted to battle, but the ultimate outcome would most likely be their deaths.

As a sudden chill gripped her, Elizabeth looked at Lucy, trying to assess what they should do. There was something in the woman's eyes . . . a spark of mischief followed by a plea of trust.

"We'll put our weapons down," Lucy said, taking several

steps forward before she bent to set her dagger next to a long, thick branch lying on the ground. The blade touched the earth for only a heartbeat before Lucy came up with the branch. In a fluid motion, she stepped toward a surprised Keddy and thrust the jagged end into his groin with all her might.

Keddy screamed, dropping his sword as he fell to his knees, clutching his most male part. With another swing of the branch, Lucy whacked Keddy on the side of the head, rendering him senseless.

"You'll pay for that!" her father roared as he charged forward with his sword. His blade arced toward Lucy but she blocked the strike with the branch and spun away as Elizabeth's father stumbled, trying to regain his balance. When he did, he let out a roar of displeasure and came at her again, but Lucy was prepared.

"Cease your attack and you might walk away unharmed," Lucy said, holding the branch before her like a quarterstaff, balancing on the balls of her feet, ready to strike, ready to defend them both.

"I'll not let you, a Douglas woman, get the best of me again!" Cursing, her father charged. His blade whistled down through the air. He spun, then came at Lucy from the side instead of down, but she was prepared and blocked the stroke.

She spun and twisted away. A heartbeat later, she attacked, striking Elizabeth's father on the leg, the shoulder, the head, until his movements were jerky and the effort to stop her hits drained him of energy. Even so, her father lunged. He caught Lucy's arm, drawing blood, but before he could step away, she jabbed her staff into his stomach.

He hissed in pain, doubled over, and his sword thumped upon the ground.

Elizabeth snatched it up. She held the heavy weapon in her own hands, pointing it at her father. She felt a surge of primitive satisfaction. "Stop this, now."

"Give me the sword, Elizabeth!"

"Never attempt to harm me or my kin again."

"I am your kin!"

"I thought so once, but I'm not so certain anymore."

Elizabeth's father's eyes glittered with anger. "They have turned you against us. They have bewitched you!"

"Nay, Father. It is you who have opened my eyes to the truth with your lies and your manipulations."

"I had hoped you would remain faithful to your clan, but it appears you serve the Douglases now?" His face twisted, contorted with anger.

Elizabeth's breath caught. Were his words true? Had she switched her allegiances and fallen for her enemy? The realization washed over her not with fear, but with acceptance. "I serve no one but God, Father." She narrowed her gaze on his face, trying to see the father she once knew in the man before her. "What is wrong with you? You've changed. You've become a—"

"Monster?" he supplied a description for her. "If I am a monster, the Douglases made me so." His eyes were cold now. "I will see they pay for their sins, and as much as it pains me, now that you are one of them, you shall pay for those sins too."

Elizabeth could only watch him hobble away with her heart in her throat. Her own father had tried to kill her, and now threatened the family who had treated her with kindness and welcomed her into their midst.

"Should I go after him?" Lucy asked with her makeshift quarterstaff still in her hands.

"Nay," Elizabeth said with a mixture of dread and anticipation. "We should head back to the carriage and make sure the coachman is unharmed and that the other men have gone."

Lucy lowered her weapon and moved to Keddy's prone form. She placed her fingers alongside his throat. "He lives. What should we do about him? He's far too heavy for us to carry."

"Leave him here," Elizabeth said. "When we return to Haddington we can send someone to collect him."

Lucy nodded and stared back toward the rowan trees. When Elizabeth continued to stand where she was, with the sword clutched in her hands, Lucy took the weapon from her and nudged her gently forward. "I cannot even imagine the sense of betrayal you must feel right now, but we must return to Haddington with all due haste before your father can regroup with his men and come after us. We were lucky this time. Let's not tempt fate any further, agreed?"

Elizabeth knew she was right, but she still couldn't quite believe her own father would sacrifice her for the sake of the Ruthven-Douglas feud. The king was right. This had to end, and it would end with her and Lachlan taking charge.

CHAPTER SEVENTEEN

ELIZABETH GREETED THE guard outside Lachlan's room with a nod before she pushed the door open and stepped inside. Lachlan stood with his battered back to her. His head was bent as he gazed into the cheery fire in the hearth. He propped one booted foot upon the grate, and stood there as still as a statue, no doubt lost in his thoughts.

There was something somber in the way he was standing. And even without looking at his face, she knew he carried the weight of what lay ahead of them on his shoulders. He stiffened suddenly and turned toward her. Sadness reflected in his features before his expression softened with a smile. "I was growing worried when you didn't arrive as planned. How did the examination go?"

"The king seemed relieved at the confirmation of my virginity, and furious as well."

"He gave you a good rousing, did he, about obeying his commands? I've been on the receiving side of many of his tirades a time or two myself," he said as he helped her remove her cloak. "Is that what kept you?"

"The carriage ran into some trouble," she said. It was the

truth, but she did not elaborate. He had enough to worry about as it was. She wouldn't trouble him with threats her father had made against them both.

"Come over by the fire." The tension that had been in his shoulders relaxed as he poured them each a glass of wine.

She accepted a glass before sitting in a chair by the hearth, allowing the flames to ward off the chill that had followed her from Hardgate Manor. "Are you improved today?" she asked, suddenly studying the contents of her glass. They both knew why she was here, and she was suddenly nervous.

"Better," he replied, taking a seat beside her. "More like myself."

She forced herself to look at him and wished she hadn't. It was difficult to be casual when he was looking at her that way, with blatant sensuality. Elizabeth hastily drank a liberal amount of her wine, praying it would calm her sudden nerves as well as the anticipation and excitement that danced in her veins.

"Elizabeth." He said the word softly as though sensing her distress. "Nothing will happen here that you do not want."

Elizabeth nodded. She set her wine aside at the unveiled passion in his eyes. That passion found an answering response within her. Her heart fluttered in her chest as he pulled her into his arms and traced his finger along the ridge of her jaw. "You have the most exquisite skin." He trailed his finger down her throat and across her collarbone. "Do you know how many times I've wanted to touch you? To cup your cheek in my palm and run my fingertips over your throat?"

"You've touched me before."

"But not like this." He ran his finger across the swell of her breasts then dipped his finger between the two lobes, making her breath catch.

A flush tinted his cheeks, his nostrils flared, and his breathing quickened. "Your breasts are quite perfect, you know."

She inhaled sharply as he lowered his head and kissed her, skillfully parting her lips and laying claim. She knew why he was kissing her—knew what his purpose was—and this time she would not stop him. He wanted her, and she wanted him.

Setting all her reservations about him aside for the last time, she kissed him in return. From this moment forward, she wanted to forget who he was and who she was and only think about the way he made her feel. Tonight, their passion would be their only guide.

She parted her lips and surrendered. A groan of pure desire escaped his lips, encouraging her. She taunted and teased, then delighted when he deepened the kiss as though he, too, was tired of fighting the passion that flared so powerfully between them.

His arms tightened around her, crushing her breasts, already peaked and tight and aching, to the hard, solid plane of his chest. His hand swept down her back, pressing her to him, then sliding lower, over her hip, to grasp her bottom and angle her hips to his so he could move against her, so he could mold her against the rigid length of his erection, let her feel and anticipate having that hard length inside her, taking her to unknown heights.

He broke the kiss and stared down at her with those bright blue eyes, eyes alive with passion—passion she'd stirred to life, passion that had turned every muscle in his body to hard-edged steel. Carefully he unlaced the back of her dress, then pulled it up over her head before removing her slippers, garters and hose. All that stood between them was her chemise.

Only the sound of their ragged breathing filled the air as with careful fingers, he lifted her chemise up and tossed it aside, leaving her naked before him. He slowly lowered his head and licked her nipple lazily.

A hot shiver moved through her. His tongue was warm and moist. His teeth closed gently on the distended pink tip, and he moved his head teasingly back and forth. Before she could get used to the sensation, he opened wide and enveloped her, devouring her as his tongue explored her in the most intimate of ways.

She was beginning to tremble, the heat between her thighs increasing until it was nearly painful, and yet she couldn't move away. She could feel the pull of his mouth with her every breath, could feel a part of her becoming a part of him. Licking a path to her other breast, he repeated his sensual seduction until finally he released her and opened his eyes, gazing at her with such pleasure that another wave of heat seared her. "Who could have known you would prove this sweet?"

Elizabeth could feel herself readying for him, feel the lust forcing away the last fragment of resistance from her mind. Waves of heat engulfed her, making her long for him in ways she'd never expected. "Lachlan—" The word was part whisper, part plea.

He straightened and she took the opportunity to unbutton his breeches, to loosen the waist and slide the garment down his legs that were almost healed of the painful red welts. All that remained of the pricker's marks were scabs that would eventually vanish for good. Following his breeches to the floor, she also removed his boots and hose, until he was also naked before her.

Lachlan lifted her and she wrapped her legs around his waist, careful to avoid his back, as he captured her lips once more. She gloried in a wave of intense pleasure at the feel of his hard, developed abdomen flexing between her thighs, fueling the fire that Lachlan had lit within her from the moment they first touched. Still locked together, he carried her across the room to the small bed and carefully laid her down. A heartbeat later, he stretched out beside her and slowly, seductively sketched his palms over her naked flesh.

Her skin burned wherever he touched, leaving trails of searing sensation across her breasts, her arms, her waist, her thighs. Wherever his hands went, his lips followed. Heat danced across her flesh. The tension built, higher and higher, until she thought she would burst from sheer pleasure.

She was breathless when he drew back to stare into her face. In his eyes she saw a fire unlike any she had seen before. "You truly are beautiful, Elizabeth. I am a lucky man." His voice was hoarse, raspy.

The way he looked at her made her feel beautiful and so many other tumultuous emotions. She wanted him with the same urgent, scorching passion with which he wanted her. That knowledge made her bold as she splayed her fingers against his rock-hard chest. She brushed his nipples with her fingertips and was rewarded with a strangled gasp of pleasure. His hooded eyes only partially concealed his smoldering gaze. "I need you to say you want me, Elizabeth."

The intensity of his passion tightened her chest. "I want you. Make love to me," she breathed, barely able to force the words from her dry throat.

He pulled her against him, then rose up on his knees and, moving over her, he settled between her thighs. His lips claimed hers again with tormenting sweetness and her body responded to the intimate sensuality of his demand. She pressed herself against his hardening body, wanting more as the flames of desire consumed her and knowing also that what came next would hurt her.

As though sensing her thoughts, he pulled back and looked into her face. "If I could take the initial pain of our joining away, I would."

"I know," she replied, bracing herself, knowing as he tensed what was going to happen.

"From the first moment I saw you on that ridge, I wanted you with an intensity that went beyond reason," he said, lifting her hips to receive him. "I even warned you that my motives for talking you away from that ledge were not altogether innocent."

"You were a rogue from the moment we first met."

"When it comes to you, aye." He entered her then, with a steady thrust.

Her body jerked and a sharp pain tore through her on a gasp, but as quickly as it came, the pain vanished, replaced by a feeling of fullness and heat. Then, guided by instinct and a heart that was overflowing, she wound her legs about his hips, drawing him deeper.

Her hands clutched at his shoulders as she thrust upward, taking as much of him as he offered her. With a low cry of wild satisfaction, she matched his rhythm, delighting as he stroked her hard and fast, slow and gentle. As soon as she grew accustomed to one rhythm, he changed it, until the tension inside her coiled tighter and tighter. His thrusts grew deeper and faster. She hovered on the brink until the tension exploded with a force that sent a fiery release through every muscle in her body.

An instant later, she could feel Lachlan spasm again and again, to shatter within her in a glorious release.

Spent, he slumped on her. She could feel his heart racing, pounding against her chest; feel the tempo of his heart echo where they were still joined.

She drew a slow, shallow breath of satisfaction, then raised a hand to his hair and, tentatively, caressed. They were married in every sense of the word now. She had truly given this man her allegiance, and she was happier than she'd ever been. He nestled against her as a quiet, tender moment ticked past.

His heartbeat gradually slowed; his breathing eased. Finally, he stirred, withdrew and moved off her only to settle against her side, his hot flesh against her own. His hands refused to release her as he played with her exposed breasts, stroking, circling, teasing as if he was afraid to let the moment end.

Never in her life had Elizabeth experienced anything like that before. She had never dreamed such satisfaction or satiation were possible as a heavy languid sensation pulsed through her blood. The physical vortex they had created had been wild, mind-bending, sense-shattering. Had she known such sensations existed, she might have been tempted to make love with him long before now.

"Will it always be like that between us?" she asked when her breathing returned to normal as she studied Lachlan's profile.

"Nay," he said. "It will only get better every single time." His lips quirked, and she recognized that smile for what it was—smug, male satisfaction.

"What are you thinking about?" she asked, unable to help herself as she realized she wanted him all over again.

He turned toward her and slid his hand to her cheek, cupping it gently. "That you are every bit as fiery and passionate in your lovemaking as you are in your everyday life."

At his broad smile, she turned her face into his hand, kissing his palm, slowly, allowing him to feel her passion.

A groan tore from his chest. He twisted onto his side and trailed his hand from her cheek, down her abdomen, until his fingers settled playfully in the curls protecting her womanhood.

"If you don't stop that, I might need to feel your passion once more," Lachlan teased.

She arched her brow. "I have no plans for the rest of the evening. Do you?"

He gave her a devastating smile and delved his fingers into her wet heat. She could feel herself readying for him again. "Shall I indulge that passionate nature of yours once more?"

Without saying another word, Elizabeth kissed him.

THE NEXT MORNING Elizabeth slowly came awake and instantly knew her life was forever altered. She and Lachlan were still curled together on the small bed. Her head rested in the curve of his shoulder, and one of her legs was lying carelessly across his, whether to keep him beside her or to offer comfort during the night she was not certain. She raised her head tentatively, but he did not stir except to release a deep, untroubled breath.

If only that were true.

Today his trial would begin. But until the bailiff came for him, Lachlan and these precious, stolen moments were all for her. Looking upon him now, she noted the changes that had taken place since last night. Gone were the lines of worry that bracketed his eyes and mouth, as was the rigid set of his jaw. He looked relaxed and so at peace even though he still remained in a prison cell of sorts. The thick, blond crescents of his lashes looked like wings upon his cheeks, and his hair was swept back from his forehead, and looked like spun gold against the whiteness of the sheets.

He was completely naked, as was she. And despite their previous night's passion, when she had thought there could be no further revelations or mysteries about his body, she discovered she was wrong. In the soft morning light, she saw him clearly in all his sheer, masculine splendor. He was perfection itself in form, but there was also evidence beyond what the pricker had inflicted upon him of past wounds. Dozens of scars, both fine and wide, threaded their way across his flesh as evidence of the many battles he had fought over the years. The pricker marks would all but vanish once they healed fully, but the stripes on his back would leave a remembrance of all he had suffered.

Elizabeth's heart swelled with both sympathy and sorrow for what he'd had to endure, and she could not stop herself from placing a tender salute upon one of the scars on his chest. As she did, another unfamiliar sensation filled her chest, replacing her sorrow with a warm tenderness.

She had thought she had loved Roland Carswell at one time in her life, but she'd been wrong. What she had experienced with him was nothing in comparison to the strange emotions that filled her when she was in Lachlan's arms. Her heart had never beat wildly out of control at the sight of him, her skin had never prickled at the sound of his voice, her body had never seemed to melt from within at his touch. All these things happened whenever Lachlan drew near, even from the first moment their eyes had met on the ledge where she had almost taken her own life.

She might not have wanted to put a name to the sensations inside her all those many days ago, but she knew now it was love. Against all odds, she was in love with Lachlan Douglas. With her heart swelling with deeper emotion than she'd ever felt before, she bent down and placed a kiss on his lips.

"Elizabeth?" His voice was slurred, but his eyes opened and fixed on her.

She meant to disentangle herself from him and rise to dress, but he tightened his arms around her and pulled her against him, refusing to let her go. "I could wake with a kiss from you every morning for the rest of my life and die a happy man." The moment he said the words, the stress that had vanished from his face returned. "I just pray that my life is longer than the next few days."

At the reminder of what still lay ahead of them, tears came to her eyes. "So many people are working on your behalf to secure your freedom. You must not lose hope. We must believe that, even with the challenges ahead, we will have a long and wonderful life together because I love you. I want to spend the rest of my days at your side as your wife, your lover, and the mother of your children. I want to grow old together and to finally put this wretched feud between our families to rest, for good."

His eyes widened as she spoke and the worry lines vanished once again. He brought his fingers up to tenderly stroke the side of her jaw. "Elizabeth, I—"

A knock sounded upon the door and the portal flew open before he could speak or they could cover themselves. King James strode into the chamber. At first, he startled at the sight that greeted him before he slowly smiled. "I am glad to see you took my command to heart, Lady March." He stared at them for a moment as Elizabeth clutched for the sheets to cover herself before turning away. "I have come to show my support for you, Lord March, by escorting you to your tribunal myself."

Lachlan recoiled as if the reality of his situation had slapped him in the face. He stiffened beneath her and shifted away from her. "That is very kind of you, Your Grace. I only hope your efforts have an impact on those gathered in the tribunal chamber."

The king's gaze returned to them, then shifted away almost as quickly again. "I shall give you a few minutes to compose yourselves. I shall wait outside." And with that he was gone, shutting the door behind him.

Silence filled the space between them as her declaration of love gave way to fear. She had finally found a purpose for her life alongside a man she loved, whom she treasured above all else, even family loyalty. But loving him also made her more vulnerable than she had been since the death of her mother. And the very serious threat upon his life suddenly tormented her with uncertainty.

What would she do if they found him guilty of sorcery? Elizabeth felt a cold chill in the hollow of her spine. Could they bribe the guard to look the other way now before the trial even started?

"Let us escape from here. Right now. This very moment. We could make a life for ourselves somewhere else."

"The king is right outside our door. I doubt he would be so kind as to release me since he hasn't up to this point. Besides, where would we go that he couldn't find us?" His eyes held a sadness that made her throat tighten. "But perhaps it is best if you return to Whittingehame. There is no need for you to suffer alongside me when the trial begins."

The air in the chamber was suddenly still, making it hard to breathe. "I cannot go. I will not. Our future is bound together."

His arms went around her and he pulled her close to his chest. She could feel the strength and warmth wrap around her for a long moment before he released her. "The king is not a patient man. And if you will not leave me, then we had best prepare ourselves for the day."

As he stood and moved to retrieve his clothing from the floor where it had fallen in their haste for each other yesterday, she said, "I believe in your innocence."

"Thank you," he said, his voice rough as he dressed.

Elizabeth took an extra moment to pin her hair up as was proper for a married lady. She readily accepted her status and was more than ready to demonstrate to the world that fact. When they had both finished dressing and prepared themselves for what lay ahead, Elizabeth held out her hand to her husband. He wrapped his fingers around hers and she hoped he could feel the love and support she extended to him without words.

The time was near. They would both meet this moment with courage and dignity. "Are you ready?" she asked.

Lachlan nodded. And together they proceeded toward whatever their future held in store.

CHAPTER EIGHTEEN

ELIZABETH WOULD NOT leave him. *Pain. Joy. Regret.* The emotions tumbled through Lachlan in a wild cataract of feeling as he stood at the front of the narrow and long room in Berwick's Old Parish church where his tribunal was about to begin. Numerous candles on the walls, windowsills, and magistrates' table spread a somber yellow glow about the room.

The guards had replaced his chains the moment he'd stepped outside Haddington Tower. The manacles rattled and clanked with every shift of his body as he stood before the magistrates. The five men dressed in scarlet robes and white wigs who were to determine his fate sat across from him: King James; John Swinton; Hugh Godfrey, the minister; the Lord Advocate, John Skene; and Lachlan's own cousin, Reid. How his cousin had convinced the king to allow him on the panel, Lachlan was not certain, but he was grateful to have at least one vote of support among those who would decide his fate.

The gallery in the tribunal chamber was filled with faces he recognized and some he did not. In the front row stood

Lucy and Elizabeth, his cousin Quinn, Cameron Sinclair, Malcolm Hamilton, Alexander Ross, and Rhys Elliot. Behind them were the fishermen they had rescued from the Firth of Forth, including Thomas Cockburn. Also present were Roland Carswell, the innkeepers from the Cairn Inn and the Buckhaven Inn, Bessie Broun, Meg and Jane Wenham, Mariam Swinton. And set off to the side was a birdcage harboring a thin, black cat. The animal turned round and round in the small space, with regular frequency letting out a mew of displeasure at being held.

They were all there. All of those whom he and Elizabeth had encountered on their journey to Whittingehame from Falkland Palace. The people who might help him prove his innocence.

Then, in the very back of the chamber stood Donald and Keddy Ruthven, as well as four others from their clan. In between the witnesses and the Ruthvens, many of the Haddington and Berwick townspeople had come to watch this latest spectacle in King James's hunt for witches and sorcerers.

"Let us proceed," the Lord Advocate said, his deep voice rising above the noise in the chamber.

The room suddenly went quiet and the air, too, felt as though it had ceased when not even the slightest breath of the wind stirred within the chamber.

"Lachlan Douglas, you are charged with multiple counts of sorcery." From the heavy record book upon the magistrates' table he read the four remaining charges against Lachlan. The fifth had been dropped after Elizabeth's examination, as promised. "We have several depositions on record that support the charges against you." He paused in his reading and looked up. "How does the accused plead?"

"Not guilty," Lachlan said without hesitation.

"Witch! Witch! You are impudent. You lie!" came shouts from the back of the chamber.

"Silence," the Lord Advocate demanded. "We shall proceed through the charges against you one by one." He cleared his throat and read: "You gave a potion to Bessie Broun of the Buckhaven Inn that sent her into convulsions as though she was possessed by demons. Witnesses saw you use magical chants to calm her." He looked directly at Lachlan. "Do you admit this is true?"

"Nay. What is true is that the morning after my wife and I arrived at Buckhaven Inn, I came downstairs and found Mistress Broun collapsed upon a table. She was unresponsive and when I placed a hand on her forehead, she was feverish. I then asked Jane Wenham to help me prepare a tonic of elderflower and peppermint that is known by many healers to reduce a fever."

"Are you stating you are a healer?" the Lord Advocate asked.

"Nay. But I know a very qualified healer who once served in the king's court." At Lachlan's reference to his cousin Vivian both Quinn and King James paled. Lachlan had to admit he did not himself have the knowledge to heal, but he would never reveal Vivian's name to the court. To do so might endanger his cousin after she had already suffered so much.

The Lord Advocate continued. "You forced this 'tonic' down the woman's throat?"

"I encouraged her to drink it. There was no force involved."

"And what was the desired outcome?"

"That her fever would reduce and then she might recover completely."

The Lord Advocate's gaze narrowed. "Did you at any time chant over this woman in order to calm her, unbaptize her, or cause the Devil to take over her soul?"

"Nay. If there was any dialogue whatsoever, it was with Jane Wenham about how to further care for Mistress Broun when my wife and I departed the inn, which we did shortly after Mistress Broun's fever seemed to abate."

The Lord Advocate set his papers on the table before him and straightened. "Bessie Broun, please come forward to the witness box and tell this court what you remember about that day."

The redheaded woman he remembered as Bessie Broun came forward and stepped into the witness box. Her features were strained and her face pale as she stood before the tribunal judges. The friendly smile she had worn so effortlessly while he and Elizabeth visited the inn had vanished.

Instead of looking at Lachlan, she gazed at her feet.

"Tell the tribunal, Mistress Broun, was there anything unusual that happened between the time Lachlan Douglas arrived at your inn and when he left?" the Lord Advocate prompted when she remained silent.

She grasped her trembling hands before her. "'Twas a fairly normal day fer me and the girls, cleanin' and cookin' fer the guests and fer travelers passin' by."

"Other than Douglas, were there any other unusual guests?"

Her frightened gaze darted to the back of the room, then back to her feet. "Two other men came in that evenin' and ate supper. They came in, ate, and left in a hurry." She shrugged. "Nae unusual fer travelers who have places tae be before nightfall."

"Do you remember becoming ill?"

She nodded. "It was shortly after the two men left."

A rumble of conversation broke out throughout the chamber.

"Did you at any time, while Lachlan Douglas was at your inn, feel threatened by him? Coerced into doing anything you did not want to do?"

Mistress Broun drew a shaking breath and looked up. "I was not myself when he supposedly gave me the potion. But Jane assures me he was only tryin' tae help when I fell ill."

"Are you now possessed by the Devil, Mistress Broun? Is he the one guiding your tongue? Because shortly after the incident happened, you gave a statement saying Lachlan Douglas had cast an enchantment over you. Are you recanting your statement?" The Lord Advocate's face reddened.

"Nay! I . . ." Mistress Broun turned a ghostly white. "I was paid tae give that testimony," she said, her voice trembling, "by the same man who returned as soon as m'laird and milady left the inn. There's nae Devil inside me. I was ill. I couldna work in my state, and an offer of coins was too hard tae resist."

Waves of shocked disbelief rippled through the chamber. And Lachlan breathed his first easy breath since his arrest as the questioning turned in his favor.

"Who was this man? Do you know him?"

She shook her head. "As I said, I was ill, and nae myself. Maybe Jane or Meg could tell ye more. They were with me when he returned."

"Thank you, Mistress Broun, you may step down." He paused to let her return to her seat before he said, "Jane and Meg Wenham, please come forward."

The two young blonde-haired women advanced. Meg, the older of the two, took her sister's hand in her own as they stepped into the witness box and faced the tribunal judges.

"What was your experience with Lachlan Douglas? Did you at any time feel threatened or as though he was there to steal your souls?"

In a quiet voice, Jane said, "Nay, good sir, m'laird was only very kind tae me, tae us, while he was there."

"Speak up, young women," the king interrupted. "We cannot hear you."

Jane startled. She clutched her sister's hand more firmly before continuing in a louder voice. "He asked me tae help him make the tonic, and showed me how tae boil the elderflower and peppermint. 'Twas all that was in the mixture, I promise ye. He even offered tae help me with some trainin' in the healing arts by findin' me a teacher."

"You testified that Lachlan Douglas had used magical chants to take over Bessie Broun's soul."

The two girls looked at each other, then darted a glance at the innkeeper and his wife before saying, "Must we say anything on that account? It could jeopardize our future."

"Aye, you must," the Lord Advocate stated. "If you do not answer my questions, I might be forced to use more forceful means of gaining your cooperation."

John Swinton smiled his pleasure.

Lachlan tensed. He would rather admit guilt where there was none, than allow Swinton to touch either of the two young women.

Meg and Jane both recoiled at the threat, but Jane nodded as she continued, "Our employer threatened tae release us if we dinna lie so he might keep the coins the two men offered us."

The innkeeper surged forward, breaking through the crowd in the gallery. "She does nae ken what she's sayin'. She's possessed by the Devil. M'laird Douglas has put her under a spell as well!"

The Lord Advocate's gaze riveted on the innkeeper as he signaled his guards to remove the man from the chamber. The innkeeper kicked and howled the entire time as they dragged him forcefully from the room. When he was gone, the Lord Advocate returned his attention to the girls before him. "How much money was offered and by whom?"

Meg straightened with bravado, as though she no longer feared what her employers might do to her if she told the truth. "He paid the innkeeper and his wife ten merks, and offered another five fer our false testimony."

"And the man? Is he here in this courtroom?"

Meg nodded, her gaze darting to the back of the chamber and to the Lord Advocate once more.

A commotion sounded at the back of the gallery. Lachlan turned to see Donald Ruthven heading for the door. He was stopped by two guards, who grabbed him by the arms and pulled him forward.

"Is this the man who paid for your false testimony?"

She nodded.

On the tribunal panel, Reid stood. "Lord Advocate, based on this new evidence that demonstrates quite explicitly that the charges against Lachlan Douglas are fabricated, may I petition the tribunal to dismiss all charges against the accused?"

Lachlan's heart skidded to a hopeful stop as the room erupted in cacophony of sound.

"Nay!" the Lord Advocate shouted over the noise. He picked up a gavel and struck the table three times, silencing the chamber.

A heavy tension seemed to scream through the room, and Lachlan's body tensed in response.

"I will hear testimony from Thomas Cockburn before anything is decided. Sit down, everyone, and let us resume our mission here." He turned his attention to Donald Ruthven, who struggled against the iron grasp of the guards. "Did you pay the innkeeper and his wife and these young women for their testimony?"

"I did no such thing. They lie under bewitchment to this sorcerer!" His fiery gaze speared Lachlan.

The Lord Advocate pressed his lips into a thin line before continuing. "Do you admit to gathering the testimony against the accused?"

"I did gather testimony, as was my duty as a concerned citizen and God-fearing man. Our own King James has spread word throughout the land that all citizens are to be vigilant in finding and prosecuting anyone and everyone who is either using sorcery or supporting those who do."

King James nodded curtly, but his jaw clenched. "My proclamations have stated as much; I will grant you that. But I will not have my purpose abused. Are you serious in your complaints against this man, or is this simply another stunt by the Ruthvens to seek revenge against an enemy?"

Donald Ruthven's face hardened into a mask of freezing

rage. "I have never been more serious, Your Grace. This man is evil. He is a sorcerer. You will learn as much if you talk with the fishermen who have testified against him."

"Did you pay them as well?" the Lord Advocate asked.

"Nay," Donald Ruthven replied with a wicked smile. "They were eager to tell me of all they had suffered at Lachlan Douglas's demonic hand."

Pandemonium erupted in the chamber while the Lord Advocate called sharply for silence. "We will continue with the witnesses to explore the charge of murder." He turned to Donald Ruthven. "You, sir, return to your place and cease these outbursts. Do you understand?"

"Aye," Donald Ruthven said with contempt in his voice.

"Thomas Cockburn, come forward." As Thomas strode to the witness box, the Wenham girls hurried to a new place in the gallery away from the innkeeper's wife at the back of the chamber.

Thomas stood tall and erect, looking far more confident than he had after his fishing vessel capsized in the Firth of Forth. The Lord Advocate picked up the papers from the desk and read aloud: "Lachlan Douglas, it is stated by witnesses that while aboard *The Golden Rose*, you caused the sea to churn, using your sorcery skills, and that ultimately you were responsible for the sinking of the fishing vessel occupied by Thomas Cockburn, Dillon Kemp, and others in this chamber, with the exception of Dillon Kemp who is deceased. When the men were subsequently rescued by the sailors aboard *The Golden Rose*, it is said that you forced them to journey on to Aberlady where you transformed yourself into your familiar, a black cat, and came forward to curse them all on their return journey to Kirkcaldy." He set the paper down and fixed Lachlan with a hard stare. "What say you to these claims against you?"

"None of that is the truth."

"Then enlighten us, please," the Lord Advocate insisted.

Lachlan nodded, relieved to finally have a chance to tell his side of the story. "Elizabeth and I boarded *The Golden Rose* from Kirkcaldy in order to escape Donald Ruthven and his men who had been following us since Falkland Palace."

The accusation against the Ruthvens caused another outbreak of conversation, which in turn caused the Lord Advocate to call for order.

When the noise settled, Lachlan said, "When we began our journey, the wind was stiff, but not a deterrent to a carrack like *The Golden Rose*. We set sail across the Firth. Halfway across, I spotted an already overturned fishing vessel with men clinging to the side. I ordered the captain to bring *The Golden Rose* alongside, and I and the sailors aboard who could swim went into the water to try and save as many as we could before they drowned. I was the one who brought Thomas Cockburn to the surface, and held him above the water until the men on the ship could hoist him aboard. After I released him, I dove back under the water in search of Dillon Kemp, but I failed to find him after many attempts below the surface of the choppy Firth."

Lachlan's gaze shifted to the fishermen who were still standing among the crowd. "Back aboard *The Golden Rose*, I bid the men go below deck to keep warm and regain their strength. There was no force of any kind applied to encourage them to go except for the constant pitching of the ship as we hit another patch of rough weather. Then once we arrived in Aberlady, we had to tender in because of the shallow harbor. The men were not forced into boats, they chose to go of their own free will. I offered to feed them and put them up at the Cairn Inn for the night, but while I was settling the horses in the stable, they returned to the shore. They are all men who know their own minds." He shrugged. "I let them go, and by no means whatsoever did I turn into a cat. My wife was waiting outside the stable with a black cat when I returned to her."

The Lord Advocate's gaze pierced Lachlan's. "Is that black cat in the tribunal chamber now?"

"'Tis the wee beast in the cage over there." Lachlan pointed to the restless animal still pacing in the confines of its temporary home.

The Lord Advocate turned to the king. "Your Grace, do you consider yourself an expert when it comes to the tricks and antics of demons?"

The king shot a scornful look at the older man. "You know that I am."

"Begging Your Grace's pardon, would you, in your expert opinion please tell the tribunal if a warlock and his familiar can exist in two separate states—man and beast—or would it be more likely for the warlock to appear as either a man or his familiar."

King James fell silent for a moment, considering, and Lachlan felt icy fear ripple through him as the entirety of the charges against him now came down to the king's opinion about the laws of witchcraft. The king scrutinized the faces of the others at the table alongside him for signs of distaste or displeasure. John Swinton's face was filled with contempt. Hugh Godfrey released a sigh of resigned disgust. A muscle in Reid's jaw began to twitch as he returned the king's glare as though compelling him to speak in favor of his cousin.

Finally, the king said, "In my learned opinion, if the animal is not a demon itself, then as a familiar, the witch or warlock must choose between the two forms—human or spirit, but not both at the same time."

The tribunal chamber erupted in chaos. Lachlan tensed as the Lord Advocate turned away from those in the chamber to discuss what happened next with the panel of judges.

The men gathered together; their heads bent so that Lachlan could not read their expressions as they discussed his fate. After several long, agonizing moments, the Lord Advocate turned back to Lachlan and those gathered in the chamber.

Swinton and Godfrey's faces held glacial hatred. Reid and King James's expressions were that of relief. "Lachlan

Douglas, Earl of March," the Lord Advocate said in a clear loud voice. "Given the fact that Donald Ruthven fabricated many of the charges against you and based on the learned opinion of none other than King James of Scotland in all matters concerning witchcraft and sorcery, this tribunal finds you innocent of all charges against you. You are free to leave."

Lachlan closed his eyes, so great was his relief. He drew an easy breath.

"Hold!"

Lachlan's breath stilled in his chest once more at the sound of Donald Ruthven's voice. The laird left his place at the back of the chamber to come forward. "Since you seem unwilling or unable to charge this man with the use of sorcery, then I would like to bring up a new charge against him. A serious charge. One that should have been addressed many years ago."

"What the devil are you playing at, Ruthven?" the king asked with a scowl. "I'll not have you dragging this out any further. It has been proven beyond a doubt that you fabricated the truth for your own devices."

"I am not playing at anything. I charge Lachlan Douglas with the murder of my wife, Janet Ruthven, twelve years ago. He is a wife-killer."

The words tumbled around in Lachlan's brain. *Murder. Wife-killer.* Released one moment and accused of a horrendous crime the next.

"Call my daughter, Elizabeth, to the witness box and ask her about the night before her mother died." There was a collective intake of breath and a low murmur that followed as those gathered speculated among themselves.

"Father, nay." It was Elizabeth's voice that pierced the haze around him.

The Lord Advocate turned to the king. "Your Grace, how would you like to proceed?"

The king's eyes were grave. "Come forward, Elizabeth Douglas, and tell this panel about that night."

CHAPTER NINETEEN

LACHLAN WATCHED ELIZABETH slowly come forward. She didn't look his way as she entered the witness box and clutched the wooden edge until her fingers turned white. Why was her father doing this to her?

One look at Donald Ruthven's face told Lachlan everything he needed to know. This wasn't to hurt Elizabeth; it was all for Lachlan. This was the ultimate revenge.

With trepidation, Lachlan watched the Lord Advocate approach. "Elizabeth Douglas, please tell this tribunal what you remember about the night before your mother died."

"I—I remember it was a long time ago and the details are not as clear as they once were." Elizabeth stole a glance at Lachlan.

He nodded encouragingly as he realized the only way for them to move forward from this moment was to get this final obstacle out into the open, even if it cost him everything he held dear. Elizabeth had told him she loved him, regardless of who he was, regardless of all that stood between their two families. Could they also move past this and into a future together? He hadn't shared his feelings with her in return because there hadn't been enough time before the king had come for him, but also because he'd wanted to wait to fully express his feelings once he had been cleared of all charges.

This final charge could prove to be his undoing. For he had been at Ruthven Castle that night . . .

"Simply tell us all that you can," the Lord Advocate encouraged in a kind voice.

"I was six years old. The night before my mother died, my father and the rest of the clan had been out on a raid. I did not know at the time that the raid had been against the Douglases." Elizabeth swallowed roughly. "When the clan returned there was much celebrating and as an adult looking back now, much indulgence in mead and whisky among the men."

When she paused, the Lord Advocate said, "Continue please."

"Late that night when everyone was abed, Lachlan Douglas managed to find a way inside our castle."

An outbreak of conversation rippled through the chamber, causing the Lord Advocate to raise his hand, demanding silence once more. "You said Lachlan Douglas was there that night."

She nodded. "He was but a lad of seven at the time, and it was the night my family murdered his mother and father in that raid."

This time when her gaze met his, it was filled with such

remorse that it rocked him clear to his toes.

"And how did you know he was present? Did he attack?" the Lord Advocate asked.

"Nay, I woke up to his presence beside my bed. He stood there beside me, staring at me."

"Did you know who he was?" the Lord Advocate asked.

"Not at the time, but when he went to my father, I soon learned he was a Douglas."

"Did he have a weapon?" King James asked.

"Was his intent to kill you in retaliation?" Hugh Godfrey demanded.

"I cannot know his intent," Elizabeth said, "but he had no weapon in his hands. He stared down at me for the longest time before he finally left my chamber."

"What happened next?" the Lord Advocate prompted.

"I slipped from my bed, and silently followed him down the hallway to my parents' chamber. He had crept inside and stood at the base of their bed, staring at them as he had done to me. My father must have sensed his presence because he woke and sat up. My mother remained sleeping."

Lachlan could see Elizabeth's hands trembling as she continued. "Lachlan did not attack, nor did my father, but I heard Lachlan curse my family," she said in a pained voice.

"What did he say exactly?" Hugh Godfrey asked with a hint of a smile.

Elizabeth's gaze shifted to the panel. Lachlan recognized the fear in her eyes and knew what she said next would not bode well for him.

"He said, 'I curse you and your family. May what you reaped this day return to you tenfold.' And with that, he disappeared from the castle."

"And how did all that affect your mother?" the Lord Advocate prompted.

Tears came to Elizabeth's eyes and rolled down her cheeks. "My father found her dead beside him the following morning."

"He cursed the Ruthvens!" John Swinton exclaimed. "He killed Lady Ruthven!"

Hugh Godfrey stood and flipped his massive Bible open. "It says here in the book of Isaiah: 'Seek unto them that have familiar spirits, and unto wizards that peep, and that mutter: should not a people seek unto their God? For the living to the dead? To the law and to the testimony: if they speak not according to this word, it is because there is no light in them.'" Godfrey looked up from the page and seared Lachlan with contempt. "There is no light in this man, therefore he is evil according to the word of God."

Shocked disbelief erupted throughout the chamber.

"He is a warlock!"

"The Devil does possess him!"

"Burn the sorcerer!"

Lachlan felt Elizabeth's gaze upon him as her tears fell all the harder. The noise in the chamber was deafening as the shouts for justice against him continued. He tried to communicate to his wife that he did not blame her for telling the truth, and he realized perhaps they should have discussed what had happened before their marriage, but he'd had no idea that she'd remembered that night until now. And she'd married him anyway.

When the noise settled down, the Lord Advocate swung toward Lachlan. "Are the events Elizabeth has confessed before this tribunal true?"

Lachlan's heart froze in his chest. He could not deny anything, and because of it, he would now be put to death for cursing the family who had murdered his parents.

"I asked you," the Lord Advocate boomed in his silence, "does she tell us the truth?"

Tearing his gaze from Elizabeth's, he said, "Aye. I cursed the Ruthvens for murdering my parents and leaving me an orphan, but I do not claim that my words held any sort of power over Lady Ruthven's death."

The Lord Advocate addressed Elizabeth once more. "Was your mother ill prior to that night?"

"She complained of a headache."

He turned his attention to Donald Ruthven. "Did anyone examine the body before her burial?"

"Nay," her father replied, "because we all knew it was Lachlan Douglas who killed her."

The Lord Advocate's brows furrowed. "Why did you not pursue charges against this man at that time? And if you suspected foul play, why did you allow your daughter to marry him?"

Donald Ruthven's shoulders stiffened. "Her marriage 'twas a business transaction between the king and queen and myself at first. But after the marriage, and when I saw the true nature of the man she had wed, I was determined to do anything to see her returned safely to her clan."

The Lord Advocate shifted to Elizabeth in what was becoming a macabre back and forth of her father's word versus her own. "Is that your wish as well—to return to the familiarity and safety of your clan? Because, as of last night, you willingly consummated your marriage, creating a bond no one but God can tear asunder."

Elizabeth's cheeks flamed red as someone in the crowded chamber released a laugh that was quickly choked. She lifted her chin and replied, "He is my husband, and what passes between a husband and wife is perfectly natural and normal."

Her father's face turned red for an entirely different reason. "You gave yourself to the man who murdered your mother?"

Elizabeth looked straight ahead, almost as if she refused to look at her father. "I do not believe he murdered my mother. It is my belief that she simply died. And while her death broke my heart, I cannot think that a seven-year-old boy in pain over the death of his own parents—whom my own family readily admits to killing—could take my mother's life with so little effort." She straightened and allowed her gaze to travel over each member of the panel. "I do not believe in curses. I will never give evil that kind of power over my rational mind."

Hugh Godfrey looked like he personally wanted to throttle her, but he remained silent.

"Thank you for your testimony, Elizabeth." The Lord Advocate motioned for her to return to her place as he turned back to the panel and the judges bent their heads together, no doubt discussing how to proceed.

Hugh Godfrey's gaze caught Lachlan's. It was filled with grim amusement before he turned back to the others. But that brief look told Lachlan everything he needed to know. He had been a free man for only a moment, and now he would die for something he had done as a child. Ruthven and Hugh Godfrey would see to that.

King James left his position at the tribunal table and moved toward one of the guards. He spoke in a low voice to the man, and when he had finished, the guard left the chamber and the king returned to his seat.

It was several moments later before the Lord Advocate stood and faced the room. "Lord Douglas, there is much to consider here, and the tribunal finds we need further testing to determine the truth."

At the mention of more 'testing' Lachlan felt his blood freeze in his veins. Did they truly mean testing or was there more torture in his future? He wasn't certain how much more he could tolerate of John Swinton's special brand of justice. If he got the chance, the man would press him beyond the point of his endurance, and as so many others before him, he would say whatever the man wanted to hear just to make the torture stop.

ELIZABETH SHUT HER eyes against the image of her husband being tortured once more. And if he was, this time it would be because of her testimony. She would send him to the hangman's noose and eventually the flames, just as had happened to the two unfortunate women at the market cross a few days before.

The shame of what she had done filled her in equal proportion to the hatred that grew for her father. He had lied to her for the whole of her life . . . and now this . . . He would take away the one person who had been honest with her from the start.

Lachlan was not her enemy; he was the man whom she loved.

A stir in the chamber brought Elizabeth out of her worrisome thoughts as the guard the king had sent out of the chamber returned with a strange-looking gadget in his hands. The king accepted what the guard offered as he stood and addressed the chamber. "I have read about this divination device in one of the books of *Occult Philosophy* written by Cornelius Agrippa and have always wanted to try it."

At the words, some of the color returned to Lachlan's

face. Was this the test the tribunal had discussed among themselves? And would they issue it in the tribunal chamber and not at the hands of John Swinton? A seed of hope took root inside Elizabeth.

The king placed what looked like a pair of shears and a sieve upon the table before him. "The Greeks used a technique called coscinomancy to determine a guilty party in a criminal offense. And since we cannot decide among ourselves whether Lachlan Douglas summoned spirits on the night of Janet Ruthven's death or not, or if he is indeed guilty of murder or if Janet's death was an unfortunate accident, we will let the coscinomancy decide."

The king motioned for both Lachlan and Donald Ruthven to take up a position in front of all those gathered in the tribunal chamber. Elizabeth drew a suffocated breath as the chamber filled with tension so thick it seemed to weigh her down. This contraption, whatever it was, would decide Lachlan's fate?

"Why am I a part of this trial now? I have done nothing but try to bring forth the truth!" Donald Ruthven's voice rose in surprise. "I refuse to be a part of this test of yours."

The king's eyes narrowed in anger. "If you've told us the truth, then you have nothing to fear. Is there something you wish to tell this tribunal? Some point you wish to elaborate upon?"

Her father pointed to Lachlan. "This man has done unspeakable things, and yet now you wish to punish me? This is ridiculous." He turned and moved toward the door, but the guards stopped him and hauled him back to the front of the chamber to stand beside Lachlan.

Her father's face was filled with menace. "Against my will I will participate, but soon you will all know the truth," he hissed. "The bastard is guilty of murder! This man destroyed my life, and my daughter's life after taking Janet away from us."

There was an edge in her father's voice that Elizabeth had never heard before and it made her heart freeze. She could see the battle going on in her father's mind as he clenched and unclenched hands that were held firmly at his sides by the guards.

Ignoring her father's outbursts, the king motioned to the panel behind him. "Reid Douglas and Hugh Godfrey, please stand facing each other before these two men." When they were in position, King James picked up the sieve and shears. "This device is said to combine the natural world with the divine. What results it gives us come directly from God."

The king placed the large shears between the two men. "Hold the shears suspended, using only your middle finger." Once the shears were in place, he positioned the wide outer rim of the sieve between the cutting edges of the blades. As soon as the sieve was in place it was impossible to keep the contraption still and it started to shift back and forth.

King James picked up a piece of parchment from which he read: "*Dies, Meis, Juschet, Benedoefet, Dowima,* and

Enitemaus." As soon as he finished, the sieve started to shudder first left, then right. "Now I will call out each of your names. The moment the guilty party is pronounced, the culprit will be instantly known to us." The king set down the parchment and straightened. "Let us proceed."

Fear and hope twisted through Elizabeth in equal measures. Either her father or Lachlan would be pronounced guilty. She feared either outcome for very different reasons. If Lachlan were guilty, he would definitely hang. If her father were guilty, then he might ultimately hang as well.

Hugh Godfrey and Reid Douglas stared at each other, locked in a battle that fate would soon decide. Each man willed the device between them to prognosticate in their favor: Reid for Lachlan, Hugh for Donald.

Elizabeth's heart was beating so hard she could feel its thunder in every part of her body.

"I present," the king said, raising his voice so that all could hear, "Lachlan Douglas and Donald Ruthven. Do as you will, oh divine device, as you are guided by God's own hand."

A hushed silence fell over the chamber, and everyone leaned forward to see the device twist left toward Lachlan and then right toward her father. It shuddered, then stopped, directly in front of her father.

The crowd gasped.

Instead of relief, Lachlan's features were still strained as his gaze sought out her own. What she read there—the sympathy and love—made her heart pound all the harder. He understood how difficult this moment was for her. This moment hurt her deeper than she had expected it to. Her father had lied to her. She didn't need a strange divining rod to tell her that. She'd come to realize almost immediately after her wedding to Lachlan, that her father would do just about anything, even use his only daughter, to continue to exact revenge upon his enemy.

His enemy, not hers.

Even so, the man was still her father. She stepped forward, and dropped into a deep curtsy. "Please, Your Grace, I beg you to have mercy upon my father. He has not been honest, but that does not mean he is beyond redemption." Elizabeth was so nervous she was shaking.

"You would have me be merciful to your father after all he has done to both you and Lachlan? That is not how justice works. And I have looked the other way with matters concerning the Ruthvens for far too long."

Donald Ruthven scowled at the king but remained silent.

Despite the fact she knew she should do the same, Elizabeth felt compelled to at least try to influence the king in some way. She looked at him and hoped he could read the sincerity in her eyes. "I can forgive my father for all he has done. Can you . . ." Her voice trailed off when she saw the king's expression harden at what he regarded as pleading. If she continued, she would only make things worse. "What will you do to him?"

The king regarded her with indifference before he addressed her father. "Donald Ruthven, you are guilty of not telling the court the truth in its pursuit of justice. And on top of that, I have had my fill of you and your Ruthven brethren over the years. I had thought the marriage of your daughter to a Douglas would end your scandalous behavior. Obviously, I was wrong. So instead of imprisoning you here so that your daughter and her husband can have any kind of life, I will grant you your freedom," he paused, as if for effect, before adding, "by banishing you to the Shetland Islands."

"*The Northern Isles of Scotland!*" Donald Ruthven cried. "I'll never find my way home from those distant shores. Might as well put me in chains here."

"You would be wise to make Shetland your new home. I hear Lerwick on the east coast of the mainland is not so bad. I will send you with a sum of money that should be enough to buy you a fresh start."

Elizabeth could see the white-hot flash of anger that swept through her father. "I won't go! You'll never make me board that ship!"

The king straightened, his own cheeks turning red. "For that outburst, I will now send one of your kin along with you. Keddy Ruthven." The king motioned that Keddy was to step forward from the back of the chamber. "You are banished along with your ex-clan leader."

Donald Ruthven's face paled as Keddy came forward.

"Who will lead the clan if I am gone?"

"You are but regent for the true clan leader, John Ruthven. How old is John at present?"

Donald Ruthven winced. "Fifteen, and too young to manage a clan with the size and complexity of the Ruthvens."

"Then I will send one of my advisors to assist him until he is fully prepared to take over," the king stated with a note of triumph in his voice.

Donald Ruthven opened his mouth to object.

"One more word out of you, Ruthven, and I will banish your entire clan."

Her father snapped his mouth closed. He stared at the king a long time until the anger faded from his eyes and was replaced by worn resignation.

Knowing he had won that battle, the king turned to Lachlan. "You are free of all charges against you, Lachlan Douglas. And while I will not banish you from Scotland, I would suggest you and your bride take a trip of some sort—perhaps travel around the continent for a time—until the anger over Donald Ruthven's banishment settles down, or until you have a Ruthven-Douglas child to bridge the divide between your two families."

In that moment, the reality of their situation hit her—Lachlan was free, her father would not be able to hurt either of them anymore, but he would be gone from her life forever.

Emotion thickened her throat as she looked at Lachlan. He tried so hard to put on a brave face, but she could see the wrenching emotions in his eyes, the regret and the sorrow over the loss of her father that matched her own. Even as horrible as her father had been to her all through her life, Lachlan realized she would mourn his loss just as much as she had mourned her mother.

"This tribunal is adjourned," the Lord Advocate announced. Slowly the crowd dispersed until only Lachlan and Elizabeth, the king, the guards, and her father and Keddy remained.

"I will give you a moment to say goodbye to your father, Elizabeth," the king said.

When they were gone, Donald Ruthven rounded on his daughter. "You never did anything right for me or the clan, Daughter. If you were a true Ruthven, you would have fought for me. I'm tempted to charge you of using witchcraft!"

Lachlan stepped forward, putting himself between Elizabeth and her father. "That is enough. I beg you not to leave your daughter with angry words that you will regret in the years ahead."

"I regret nothing, except having a daughter instead of a son," Donald Ruthven growled.

Lachlan straightened. He stood with his legs widened and by placing his hands on his hips, he made himself appear larger than he usually was. "Whether you want to hear this or not, I forgive you for all you put me through," Lachlan said as he slipped his arm around her waist. "I will show that forgiveness every day as I care for your daughter."

"I forgive you as well. I know you are angry and do not really mean what you say. At least, I hope not," Elizabeth said, suddenly seeing her father as her equal and no longer through a child's eyes. He was a man filled with strength and faults. Perhaps in a new location he could find a place for himself and use his strengths for the betterment of all those whom his life would touch. For an instant she felt a pang of regret that she would not be a part of that new life, then a warm ripple of contentment flowed over her as she turned to gaze at Lachlan. Her life was here with her husband.

Lachlan held her tight against his side as the guards led Keddy and her father away and the king followed, leaving the two of them alone.

"I won't see him ever again, will I?" Elizabeth whispered.

"None of us know what the future holds," Lachlan replied as he bent and placed a kiss atop her head. "I, for one, would like very much to put some distance between myself and Berwick."

Just then the yowl of displeasure filled the chamber. "The cat! They left the cat behind." She turned to him; her eyes wide. "We cannot leave him here. Can we please take him back to Whittingehame with us?"

"As a once-suspected warlock, you wish me to harbor a black cat in my castle?"

Elizabeth frowned. "You and I both know he has no great powers other than ridding you of vermin."

"Very true." He sighed. "As you wish. We shall give him a new home."

She smiled her pleasure, but a heartbeat later that smile faded as she looked about the chamber one final time. "Before we leave, I want you to know I didn't want to testify against you. I do not believe you killed my mother. I wouldn't have said anything if my father—"

"I was angry when I came to Ruthven Castle that night," he explained quietly. "I wasn't sure why I was even there, other than that I had to see with my own eyes the man who had killed my parents. When I stumbled into your chamber instead of your parents' by mistake, I watched you sleep for a time before you woke. And once I looked into your eyes, I knew I could never do to you what had been done to me." His lips twisted. "I left you then and went to your parents. Again, I was angry, but instead of harming them, I wanted fate to take its course. Today it did with your father. Your mother . . ." He paused as his gaze dropped to the floor. "I'm so sorry, Elizabeth."

"I don't believe in curses," she said, "or witchcraft or sorcery. You did not hurt my mother. As I said, she had a headache that night. I truly believe something happened in the night that stole her from us—something normal and natural—something beyond our control." She paused and swallowed back the tears she could feel burning at the back of her throat. "I should be the one apologizing. My family has been nothing but trouble for you."

He looked at her with a smile in his beautiful blue eyes. "Some things are worth a great deal of trouble." He lifted her chin with his finger and searched her face. "You are worth everything. You are the prize I always wanted and never thought I would have. I love you, Elizabeth. I have loved you from the first moment we met, so many years ago. And I loved you more when I saw you on the cliff, and every day after that, my heart was filled with joy as we put our families' past behind us to make a life of our own."

Everything they had been through in the last week suddenly came back to her. Without either of them knowing, the pain and the turmoil of those events had shaped their future, inexorably interwoven their paths, leading them to right here and now. She smiled at him, allowing him to see all the love in her heart. "True love and true forgiveness are gifts given to those who survive the peaks and the valleys of this life."

He bent and kissed her tenderly then whispered against her ear. "You and me, not a Ruthven and Douglas, but simply two souls uniting as one."

Elizabeth's chest suddenly felt too small for her heart. She didn't know love could feel like this—so filled with joy and magic.

As though reading her thoughts, he pulled back and smiled. "I am no warlock, but I do believe in magic . . . the magic of love, and forgiveness, and the magic of you, my love."

He held out his hand to her then. "Are you ready for the next part of our adventure?"

She curled her fingers around his. "I'm ready."

CHAPTER TWENTY

L ACHLAN AND ELIZABETH returned to Whittingehame
Castle that night along with the balance of the king's
Magnificent Seven, who had insisted on escorting them
home to prevent further incident. When all were settled in
their chambers, Lachlan presented Elizabeth with a gift.

"What is this?" she asked, staring down at the folded
piece of red silk with what felt like a small object inside.

"Open it up to find out," he said with a grin.

When she pulled the silken edges of the cloth back, she
felt tears come to her eyes. "My mother's ring. How did you
accomplish this?"

He took the ring from her hand and slid it onto her right
finger where she had worn it for years. "I found the guard
you traded it with and offered him something of much
greater value for its return. Every man has a price."

"And what was his?"

A smile touched Lachlan's lips. "A crofter's share of our
land here at Whittingehame for his wife and family."

She smiled in return. "That was kind of you."

"Nay," Lachlan said, his gaze once more on her face. "I

sacrificed nothing and received treasure in return."

Treasure. She'd never been called such before.

"Now that that is done." Lachlan held out his hand to her. "I have been dying to hold you in my arms since we left Berwick. Will you come with me, Elizabeth, to our bed?"

Elizabeth could feel her heart start to pound just looking at him, at the smile that brought a flare of passionate intensity to his eyes. "Aye," she said as she placed her hand in his.

He led her up the stairs, down the hallway, and into their bedchamber. He shut the door behind them and she stood there, suddenly fascinated at the sight of him as he removed his boots and sword. Once he set those aside, he began to remove the tartan he'd changed into after he'd bathed upon their arrival home. He'd said it was so he could leave all traces of Berwick behind him. When his tartan pooled on the floor at his feet, he stripped off his shirt and threw it aside, until he stood naked before her. Her heart stumbled as she noted his pricker's marks had faded to only pink spots that would soon be gone entirely.

And more than anything she wanted to touch his skin, blemished or not, to close her fingers on the golden, springy thatch on his chest, rub her palms over the smooth, hard, musculature of his shoulders, and try to cleanse from him the memory of all he had suffered, replaced with sensations of pleasure and passion.

The shutters were open, letting in the sweet heather-scented air as well as the moonlight that bathed him in a silvery glow, delineating each feature of his face, the tough, sinewy strength of his shoulders and his thighs. His every muscle was tense, and his manhood boldly aroused.

Suddenly, she couldn't breathe as the air in the room seemed heavy and vibrating with the same arousal she saw in him. She came toward him then, unable to resist him any longer, moving closer to him until she felt the heat of his body against her own. And when she looked up at him, he bent his head down and kissed her. Softly at first, just a brush of his lips against hers, until she heard herself release an appreciative sigh, and with a groan of his own, he took her mouth, urging it open, as though he needed to taste her very essence.

His hands came up to pull the pins from her hair, and he let them drop as he slid his fingers through her hair, fanning the heavy length across her shoulders and down her back. His mouth moved from hers and traced the sensitive flesh of her throat. He dragged down the sleeves of her gown, revealing her breasts.

The warm night air caressed her bare skin, tingling and curiously erotic. Then she felt his tongue, hot and wet, circling her nipples, urging them to taut, painful peaks until she nearly cried out with longing.

His hands moved behind her to release the fastenings of her gown. As his fingers brushed her flesh she inhaled sharply at the sensation. Her gown fell into a pool of damask at her feet. He bent his head down again and pressed the gentlest of kisses to her shoulder as his hands moved to push her chemise down the length of her body to settle atop her dress.

Elizabeth gasped at the loss of his nearness as he moved briefly away before returning with his tartan. He draped the cloth across the shoulder he had kissed, and wound the length about her waist, allowing the ends to trail upon the floor. He lifted her hand and placed it on his chest. She felt the thunder of his heart beneath her palm.

"Now you are truly my lady and I want you," he said softly. "I don't think I've ever wanted you more. It's important to me that you know it was thinking about you, about this, that kept me sane during—"

She kissed the words away. There was no need to say them. She knew he spoke of his time in the gaol, and at the hands of John Swinton. "Turn around," she said softly.

He tensed. "The wounds will fade with time," he said, his voice tight.

"This moment for us is a time of healing. Let me heal you, Lachlan, to replace the horrors with new memories."

After a slight hesitation, he turned and she saw the welts and cuts on his back had faded to slivers of pink and purple. The open wounds were no longer bleeding, but scabbed and healing.

Slowly, reverently, she bent and pressed her lips lightly to each mark. "I love you. I need you. Please be mine, forever," she said the words in a litany until she no longer saw the wounds, but instead felt his strength, his hardness, his heat.

When she paused, he turned around and simply held her gaze with hope burning brightly in his eyes. "I am yours and you are mine with all our faults and all our glory."

Tears of happiness she'd never thought to feel filled her eyes. The same emotion swelled in her chest and filled her heart to overflowing.

He kissed her again, a long deep kiss that stirred the flames between them to life once more. When he broke the kiss, he lifted her in his arms and carried her to the bed. He laid her down on the soft coverlet, before joining her there, kissing the sensitive flesh behind her ear, following it with his tongue, stoking the fires as he trailed kisses along her collarbone and between her breasts. She arched against him with a silent moan, communicating her need.

He understood and gently unwrapped the tartan from around her before he knelt between her legs, parting her thighs. His arousal pressed against her as he entered her slowly, carefully, until he filled her completely. She clutched at the coverlet, so intense were the sensations rippling through her. His very slowness, deliberateness was unbearably erotic and sensual. She felt the hardness of his body against her, felt him sink into her, gently increasing the rhythm until Elizabeth felt pressure building, slowly, intensely.

She ran her hands over the smoothness of his heated shoulders and back, until she locked her legs around his hips and rocked with him. When she opened her eyes to look at him, her breath caught. He gazed down upon her with eyes darkened with passion, his throat sinewy with the strain of holding back.

Elizabeth rocked against him, feeling the slide of his body against her own, reveling in the exotic sensation of his chest hair brushing her sensitive nipples until the pressure inside her built, swirling, rising, filing her body and her soul until they scaled that peak, celebrating the beginning of a new life together. Love drove them, held them, and enfolded them until it felt as though the sun, the moon, and the stars were shining upon them all at once.

When at last they slumped together with warmth and satiation heavy in their veins and their heartbeats slowly returning to a normal rhythm, Lachlan shifted his head and pressed a kiss to her temple. "We were destined to be together, my dear Elizabeth. No matter the obstacles that stood between us. We made it to this moment, and if I am not mistaken, we have accomplished yet another task the king has set before us."

She leaned up on her elbow and stared down into her husband's face. "What are you speaking of? What task have we accomplished for the king here in our bedchamber?"

He lowered his head and placed a kiss upon her abdomen. "A bairn. I am convinced our joining has brought forth a new life."

"You cannot know such things."

"But I do," he said with a laugh. "Trust me, you will

come to know the truth very soon. What we just experienced was the closest thing to magic upon this very earth."

Elizabeth smiled, still feeling branded by the taste of him on her lips and the feel of him against her flesh. "Then let us surround ourselves with magic once again."

And so, they did.

CHAPTER TWENTY-ONE

THE NEXT MORNING, Lachlan and Elizabeth arrived in the great hall to find at table the others who had returned to Whittingehame with them, breaking their fasts. At their entrance, Lachlan's fellow warriors gathered around them. With great joy, Lachlan introduced Elizabeth to them all. They were greeted with hugs from Lucy, and his cousins greeted her with a kiss on the cheek and him a stout pat on the back.

"Thank you all for traveling with us last night," Lachlan said to the group of men and one woman. "After such an eventful week prior, it was comforting to know we would have an uneventful return home."

Alexander Ross's lips quirked. "Your future is anything but settled. What will you do now that the king has bid you to leave Scotland for a time?"

"Where will you go?" Rhys Elliot asked.

When Lachlan didn't immediately reply, Cameron Sinclair came to stand before him and Elizabeth. "I might have a solution for you, if you will accept it."

Lachlan's brows drew together. "Elizabeth and I really

haven't discussed our options yet."

"Hear me out," Cameron said. "As you left Ravenscraig, heading for the harbor in Kirkcaldy, I saw the way both of you looked at the sea. There is a bit of a sailor in each of you if I am not mistaken." He looked to Elizabeth for confirmation or denial of his claim.

"I cannot deny that I felt an inner restlessness as well as a sense of peace aboard *The Golden Rose*. I've been so sheltered all my life. There is great attraction to discovering just how big and how wonderful this world truly is."

Cameron turned to Lachlan with an arched brow. "And do you feel the same?"

He put his arm around Elizabeth and held her tight against his side. "I could not agree with my wife more."

Cameron nodded. "Then please accept as a wedding gift my carrack *Destiny's Song* and a crew to go with her. She is a fine three-masted ship with twelve cannons, and she'll see you safely wherever you choose to set sail."

Both Lachlan and Elizabeth gaped at him in amazement. Lachlan recovered his voice first. "That is truly kind, Cameron, and we are honored by your thoughtfulness, but that is far too generous a gift."

Cameron's features darkened. "Are you not my brother-in-arms?"

"Aye," Lachlan responded.

"Would you not give me whatever you had if I needed it?"

Lachlan could not deny the truth of that. "Aye, without hesitation."

"Then accept what I offer you—a chance to be free from Scotland for a time, surrounded by an ocean that will keep you in relative safety, and take you wherever your hearts desire."

Lachlan covered Elizabeth's hand with his. "We are starting a new life, my love. What would you say if we continued that journey upon the sea?" His gaze searched her face.

She smiled. "My heart and my home are where you are. I think I would like sailing across the sea at your side."

"And the bairn? Do you think you could be with child while we are nowhere near land?"

Lucy's eyes widened. "You are with child?"

"Only my husband seems to think so," Elizabeth said with a soft chuckle.

"Hmm," Lucy said, studying his wife's face. "Your skin is glowing and there is a bloom of something in your face."

"Only time will tell on that matter." Elizabeth's cheeks pinkened. "Aye, Lachlan, I will do perfectly well as your wife or the mother of your children on land or at sea."

"Then the ship is yours if you accept it," Cameron said.

"We accept it," Lachlan said, taking Elizabeth's hand in his. "And the rest of you must promise to stay hale and hearty while we are away."

"We promise," they replied in unison before they returned to their breakfasts.

When they were seated again, Lachlan slipped his fingers beneath her chin and angled her head back for his kiss. It was a long, slow, deep kiss—a kiss of thankfulness that they were together and safe, a kiss of hope for all the days that lay ahead, and a kiss of promise for all the other kisses their future held. When Elizabeth could speak once more, she asked, "When will we leave?"

"Is tomorrow too soon to head to Kirkcaldy? No sense in setting down roots here only to rip them up shortly after."

"I agree," she said with a sad smile.

"What is it, my love?"

"Do you think our life will ever be one of calm serenity?"

"Is that the life you want?"

She squared her shoulders as she smiled up at him. "Not really. I have a feeling every day with you will be a new adventure, for the rest of our lives."

Lachlan laughed, content with the feel of the woman he'd always wanted in his arms. God had answered his prayers. For that fact, Lachlan was grateful. "Life for us will always be filled with twists and turns, storms and sunlight, moonless nights and star-filled skies. Would you be happy with anything less?"

"Never." Elizabeth put her arms around his neck. "Your brothers-in-arms made you a promise. Will you make one to me as well?"

"Do you not know by now I will do anything for you?"

She arched a brow. "That is not an answer."

"Aye." He smiled. "What would you have of me?"

"Promise to never think of me as your enemy again."

"You are my life, my heart, my soul. I think I can safely promise you that." And with those words he kissed her.

The End

Author's Note

Lachlan Douglas's experiences as an accused warlock in *A Temptress in Tartan* are based on the experiences of hundreds of real-life accused so-called witches and warlocks. In sixteenth, seventeenth, and early eighteenth-century Scotland, witches were hunted with fanatical zeal, some of which was a result of a reappraisal of religious values, practices, and attitudes as the Reformed church took hold of Scotland. Another force that exacerbated the supposed rooting out of all evil in Scotland was the *Witchcraft Act* of 1563.

Queen Elizabeth I signed the act into law in England, and Mary Queen of Scots was encouraged by her advisors to do the same but with two differences. It was those differences in the law that proved disastrous for Scottish witches. The first was that witches were considered heretics, and therefore subject to the death penalty. The second was that the law declared those who refused to accept that witches and witchcraft existed and those who consulted, aided or abetted a person suspected of witchcraft were equally guilty of the crime. This technically denied the Scottish legal profession any chance of success in the defense of a witch.

King James VI fanned the flames of witch-fever with his own superstitions. He encouraged religious leaders and civic leaders to cleanse their kirks and villages of all who were suspected agents of Satan. The most common suspicions concerned disruptions with livestock, crops, storms, disease, property and inheritance, sexual dysfunction or rivalry, family feuds, marital discord, step-parents, sibling rivalries, and local politics.

Trial by local commission was by far the most common practice in Scotland. Using local commissions freed the central court and circuit courts from unmanageable case-loads. They also offered a convenient solution for dealing with groups of witches, since inevitably when a witch was apprehended and tortured, she usually informed on other 'witches' in the district.

The methods used to try witches were simple. Before a secular trial took place, the kirk session, with its ministers and elders, examined the suspect. Usually a witch pricker was called in to search the victim's body for a Devil's mark. These humiliating body searches were only a foretaste of the tortures to come. The most common marks were warts or moles that when pricked with a long, thin brass pin, often inserted to the depth of three to four inches into the flesh, failed to produce either pain or blood.

Once it was determined that the victim was a witch, they were either forced to sign a confession written in Latin that they usually could not read, or they were subjected to further torture in order to coerce them to reveal the names of other witches in their presumed covens. The forms of torture used were so horrific, victims usually admitted to anything just to make the agonizing pain stop.

It is not known for certain how many men and women were executed during the witchcraft trials in Scotland, but the total is estimated to be between 3,000 to 4,000 between 1560 and 1707. Only the most fortunate were able to escape certain death once charged. If they escaped prosecution it was because they either survived their torture without confessing, were delivered by a "seer" who could look into the accused's eyes and see a special mark proving their innocence, or by some strange test like the one used to free Lachlan Douglas.

Coscinomancy is a form of divination that was used in ancient Greece, medieval and early modern Europe, and seventeenth-century New England to determine a guilty  party in a criminal offense. Cornelius Agrippa wrote about this technique in the first volume of his *Three Books of Occult Philosophy*, the *Opera Omnia*. Using this technique, a sieve was suspended from shears in such a way that the cutting edges of the blades made contact with the outer rim of the sieve. The shears were held by two middle fingers or by a string, making it almost impossible to keep the sieve still for any length of time and thus ensuring a prognostication.

King James wrote about this technique for revealing a guilty party in his book, *Demonology*, which was a philosophical dissertation on necromancy and the historical relationships between the various methods of divination used from ancient black magic.

During the days of the witch hunts, familiars were said to be given to witches by the Devil. They were, in essence, small demons that could be sent out to do a witch's bidding. Although cats, especially black ones, were the suspected favored vessel for such a demon to inhabit, dogs, toads, owls, ravens, and other small animals were sometimes used.

The facts about the witch hunts and witchcraft trials in the *All the King's Men* series are difficult to process in a modern era where human life is valued and respected. The books highlight the brutal treatment meted out to those accused of practicing the black arts. I chose to make my hero suffer some of that torture in this work in order to illustrate what did happen during the witch trials. However, Lachlan's torture was minimal compared to what others would have suffered in these historical times in order to gain confessions, which made ridiculous and outrageous claims.

The books in this series are meant to draw attention to the farcical and absurd beliefs held not only by the uneducated population, but also the upper class. We will never know the true number of victims caught up in the witchcraft trials, but what is certain is that several thousand men and women went to their deaths unnecessarily.

There are no memorials to those who perished in Scotland, other than the odd placard or place name that marks an execution spot or where supposed witches held their covens and Sabbats. However, through stories like those in the *All the King's Men* series, it is my hope that the lessons of the past are remembered, and that we, as a people, never forget the best part of being human is our humanity toward others.

All the King's Men

Men of unequaled spirit, strength, and courage who were chosen by King James the VI as his Magnificent Seven.

Quinn Douglas

Reid Douglas

Lachlan Douglas

Alexander Ross

Cameron Sinclair

Rhys Elliot

Malcolm Hamilton

If you enjoyed *A Temptress in Tartan*,
you'll love the next book in….

All the Kings Men series

Book 1: *Seven Nights with A Scot*

Book 2: *Romancing the Laird*

Book 3: *A Temptress in Tartan*

Available now at your favorite online retailer!

About the Author

Gerri Russell is the award-winning author of historical and contemporary novels including the Brotherhood of the Scottish Templars series and *Flirting with Felicity*. A two-time recipient of the Romance Writers of America's Golden Heart Award and winner of the American Title II competition sponsored by *RT Book Reviews* magazine, she is best known for her adventurous and emotionally intense novels set in the thirteenth- and fourteenth-century Scottish Highlands. Before Gerri followed her passion for writing romance novels, she worked as a broadcast journalist, a newspaper reporter, a magazine columnist, a technical writer and editor, and an instructional designer. She lives in the Pacific Northwest with her husband and four mischievous black cats.

Thank you for reading

A Temptress in Tartan

If you enjoyed this book, you can find more from all our great authors at TulePublishing.com, or from your favorite online retailer.

11087245R10173

Made in the USA
Monee, IL
06 September 2019